Lone Wolf

ALSO BY EDO VAN BELKOM

Wolf Pack

Lone Wolf

EDO VAN BELKOM

Tundra Books

Text copyright © 2005 by Edo van Belkom

Published in Canada by Tundra Books,
481 University Avenue, Toronto, Ontario M5G 2E9

Published in the United States by Tundra Books of Northern New York,
P.O. Box 1030, Plattsburgh, New York 12901

Library of Congress Control Number: 2004117248

Library and Archives Canada Cataloguing in Publication

Van Belkom, Edo
Lone wolf / Edo van Belkom.

ISBN 0-88776-741-9

I. Title.

PS8593.A53753L66 2005   jC813'.54   C2004-907145-9

We acknowledge the financial support of the Government of Canada
through the Book Publishing Industry Development Program (BPIDP)
and that of the Government of Ontario through the Ontario Media
Development Corporation's Ontario Book Initiative. We further
acknowledge the support of the Canada Council for the Arts and the
Ontario Arts Council for our publishing program.

ONTARIO ARTS COUNCIL
CONSEIL DES ARTS DE L'ONTARIO

Cover: David Parkins
Design: Cindy Elisabeth Reichle

Printed and bound in Canada

This book is printed on acid-free paper that is 100% recycled,
ancient-forest friendly (40% post-consumer recycled).

1 2 3 4 5 6   10 09 08 07 06 05

To Dr. Sheldon Katz,
family physician and friend.

Chapter 1

The morning mist hung heavily in the air like smoke. As the pack ran through the forest, their fur netted the moisture, wetting them, but never soaking them to the skin. The ground was soft and damp, smelling of nature and new life, as if the earth itself were a living thing.

As the pack ran, Tora led the way for her three brothers, never venturing far from the trail. Harlan followed her closely, struggling only slightly to keep up. He'd always been the runt of the litter, but he'd been enjoying a growth spurt the past few months and now was just an inch shorter than Tora in human form and only a few pounds lighter as a wolf. By spring he'd be bigger than her, and stronger too, or at least that was his hope. Behind Harlan, Noble kept a comfortable pace, nipping at Harlan's heels every so often to ensure his smaller brother kept up with the others. Noble could easily have been out front, the lead being his usual position among the pack, but he was happy to follow every so often, relieving himself of the burden of responsibility for his three siblings.

Bringing up the rear was Argus, by far the largest and strongest member of the pack. Argus too, could have been up front if he'd wanted, and even Noble knew enough not to challenge such a thing if Argus had his mind set on it. But today Argus was content to be last. He'd been similarly content with the position all week, and it didn't look like his feelings would be changing any time soon.

The truth was that Argus had seen this part of the forest many times before, and he'd become bored with it. For weeks he'd been wondering what lay beyond the pack's usual hangouts, beyond the familiar part of the forest. What, for example, was the ground like farther up the mountains? And at the top, or perhaps even over them? What was there for him to discover? He was nearly sixteen years old, and he'd yet to see the ocean in anything other than pictures or on TV.

Argus hung back, keeping his siblings within sight through the mist and fog, doing little to close the gap between them. Who cared if he fell behind or even found himself alone in unfamiliar forest? Argus would welcome some new territory to explore. What challenges awaited him beyond the town of Redstone? Strange beasts, perhaps ready to be hunted and felled, torn apart by talons and teeth, their blood rich and red and tasting like . . .

Argus did his best to concentrate on the pack and what had become a boring run through the forest. It wasn't a good idea to dwell on such things as making meals of the other animals in the woods. Too much thought on the subject, a single taste of fresh hot blood, and he'd develop a liking for it. Then, almost like a drug addict, he'd want more and more, never satisfied until the bloodlust overtook him, or he was finished off by another beast that was bigger, stronger, or smarter than he was. There were countless animals that he could kill, and only a few that might be able to kill him, but that didn't mean they weren't out there. If he preyed on the smaller animals, the bigger ones would find him, of that he had no doubt.

Argus raised his head and looked up the trail for the other members of the pack. He could see the branches and grass along the sides of the trail moving slightly to denote their passing, but other than that there were no signs of his siblings anywhere. He slowed and bent to sniff the ground. Their scent was fresh, and the flicking and bending of the blades of grass told Argus that they were no more than a few seconds ahead.

He slowed yet again, allowing himself to fall even farther behind. Argus preferred to be alone more often of late. He wasn't sure why, but there was a feeling within him – almost a certainty – that he would be leaving the pack before long.

Just then, the hair along the back of Argus's head stood up. There was something on the trail ahead that wasn't a member of the pack. He sensed something about the presence that made him wary.

Argus stopped in his tracks, moving off the trail and finding cover behind a stout redwood that would conceal his position no matter which form he was in. And then he waited. He couldn't see anything through the mist or between the trees, but there was something there, he was sure of it. He could hear it rustling through the brush and padding lightly over the humus. It was a faint sound like that of a small deer, or perhaps even a dog leading a hunter. The thought of a hunter on the pack's trail caused Argus's fur to bristle with fury.

And then he saw it shrouded in fog, or at least he thought he saw it. At that moment, Argus had been sure that what he had seen was real. But later, upon discussing it with Ranger Brock and his brothers and sister, he would become uncertain of himself; doubting his own eyes and wondering if the madness he feared wasn't already creeping inside his head.

But all that came later. Right now he saw a naked man move between the trees in the distance, almost like a ghost walking after midnight. He saw flashes and glimpses of the being for several moments before it moved out into the open and stepped across the path, allowing him to discern the thing's faint outline.

Argus didn't know what to make of the sight. He'd seen people in the forest often enough, hikers usually, or the occasional ranger doing some survey or patrol, even television journalists and their crews taping things they weren't supposed to. But while intrusive, those humans were to be expected. Furthermore, they were, more often than not, fully clothed when they walked through the woods. This man – he could tell that much from the outline – was completely naked. Not only that, but his hair was long, thick, and matted, and his beard was equally thick and tangled. He looked dirty too, with dark patches staining his skin like camouflage. But even his nakedness wasn't the strangest thing about the man. What really struck Argus as unnatural was the way he walked, with his head held high and his chest thrust out as if there was an air of confidence about him.

It was as if . . . he belonged in the forest.

And then, just as quickly as he'd appeared, the man was gone. Argus blinked several times, trying to decide if what he'd seen was real or just a trick of the light. Already there was a seed of doubt in his mind.

Argus's body was jostled slightly and he turned to see Noble beside him. No doubt the pack had noticed that he'd fallen behind and Noble had come back to get him. The group stayed together, no matter how much one of them felt like breaking away.

Noble gestured up the path with his head, suggesting that Argus needed to get moving. Argus nodded, then started up the trail. He slowed at the spot where he thought he'd seen the man, but all he could detect was the scent of wolves on the ground.

5

Noble gave Argus a second push, and together the two of them hurried to catch up to the others.

Their run finished, the pack returned to Ranger Brock's home in plenty of time for breakfast. The bus that took them to school wouldn't arrive for another half hour and the ranger's wife, Phyllis, would insist that they have a full meal before beginning their day as humans.

That morning's meal consisted of Ranger Brock's favorite breakfast sausages, which they'd already had three times that week. Among the pack, Tora and Harlan liked sausages best. Noble seemed not to care much about them either way, but Argus had had his fill. Not only were sausages made in some factory from scraps of leftover and discarded meat, these particular sausages had been flavored with maple sugar and honey. Argus found the combination disgustingly gross, but was too respectful of Phyllis to say so.

"Don't you want any sausages?" she asked, noticing that Argus hadn't spooned any onto his plate.

"No, thank you," Argus said. "I guess I'm not hungry." That much was true. While he normally ate heartily, the incident out on the trail had taken away much of his appetite.

"More for me!" Harlan said, scooping four sausages out of the pan before Argus changed his mind.

"Are you sick?" Ranger Brock asked, taking a gulp from his big black BC Lions coffee mug. Phyllis placed the palm of her right hand on Argus's forehead.

Although her hand felt cool against his skin, Argus doubted there was anything physically wrong with him. "I'm fine."

"You're a little warm," she said, rubbing her fingers together to feel for any moisture. Then she placed the back of her hand against Argus's cheek.

"Really, I'm fine!" Argus repeated.

"Are you sure? I could get the ranger to take you into town to see Doctor Katz."

"Wouldn't be a problem," said the ranger. "It's on my way."

Doctor Katz was new in town and was as eager as he was young. Every time Argus or one of the others paid him a visit, he was always asking them questions about their hair and skin, curious as to how the four of them were brothers and sister all the same age, but as unalike from each other as the four seasons. He obviously suspected they were somehow different, and seemed determined to find out one way or another. It was probably best to avoid visits to the doctor unless they were absolutely necessary.

So instead of answering with another "I'm fine," Argus simply grabbed two sausages off Harlan's plate and slid them into his mouth.

"Hey!"

Phyllis's face brightened and her lips curled into a smile.

The sausages didn't taste all that bad, Argus concluded, grabbing the last of them out of the pan for himself.

"That's better," Phyllis said, giving Argus an approving rub on the head.

The ranger finished his coffee and slid his chair away from the table. "Well, I've got to go," he said.

"Already?"

"They want the survey finished by the end of the week. I think they've even got Sergeant Martin and a couple of his officers pitching in to get it done." Ranger Brock had been helping with a land survey being conducted by the Forestry Service, and had been putting in a string of twelve-hour days the last week or so. He hadn't said much about the survey, but it was obvious to everyone there was something about it that concerned him. "Have a good day at school," he said. "I'll see you tonight."

Phyllis filled the ranger's thermos with coffee, then followed him out the door to see him off.

"*Are* you okay?" Noble asked Argus the moment Phyllis and Ranger Brock were gone.

"I'm fine," Argus snapped. Then he sighed and said, "I don't know."

Noble, Tora, and Harlan all stopped eating for the moment and looked at their brother.

"Did any of you notice anything strange out on the trail this morning?"

"It was wet," Harlan stated. "Lots of rain and fog, even for that time of day."

Argus shook his head. "That's not what I mean."

"Then what *do* you mean?" Tora asked.

"Did you see anything *strange* out there?"

Noble pressed him. "Strange like what?"

Argus gave the question some thought. He wanted to tell them what he'd seen, but the truth was that he wasn't sure anymore. None of the others had noticed anything odd this morning, or even sensed anything unusual out on the trail. Should he tell them that he'd seen some sort of ghost or phantom? If he had to put a name to it, that's what he'd call it, but telling them that would only get him laughed at, especially by Harlan who was always up for anything that made his big brother look foolish.

In the end, Argus cracked a smile and said, "*Strange . . .* like Harlan being able to keep up with Tora the entire way."

Tora chuckled. Noble laughed out loud. Harlan's brow furrowed and his lips turned down in a frown. He gave Argus a punch in the arm and said, "Not funny!"

Argus returned the punch, catching Harlan's right bicep with the point of a knuckle.

"Ow!" Harlan cried.

"C'mon, I didn't hit you that hard," Argus reasoned.

"You did too," Harlan said, raising his fist to return the blow.

Just then, Phyllis stepped back into the kitchen. "That's enough, Harlan. Stop picking on your brother."

"But I didn't do anything!"

Argus took the opportunity to wince and rub his shoulder, making it look as though Harlan had already hit him with a hard blow that would leave him sore for days.

"Sorry, Argus," Phyllis said, "but Tora's the actor in the family."

Argus straightened his body, the pain in his arm suddenly gone.

"Now get going, all of you. And try to stay out of trouble if you can."

They all nodded as they went out. Phyllis said that last bit every day before they left the house, but it didn't seem to help any. Trouble had a knack of finding the four, no matter how they tried to avoid it.

Chapter 2

Redstone Secondary was bustling with more students than the town had residents. Busloads of teenagers trucked to school each morning from the surrounding towns, making it the place to be if you were between the ages of thirteen and eighteen. A fairly modern building, it consolidated all of the smaller schools into one super educational facility, funded with a large enough budget to acquire everything the kids needed to compete in the world outside Redstone. This was especially important, since few students hung around Redstone after graduation, opting instead to spread their wings and give Vancouver, Edmonton, or Calgary a try. Some of them even ventured as far as Toronto, pursuing careers in music or acting or one of the other arts. The pack had sometimes wondered what they might do after they'd finished high school. Harlan had his sights set on some sort of computer science degree, or information technology as they called it these days. Tora was a venturesome spirit and often talked about stage acting in Toronto, or perhaps in Stratford. Argus would likely stay put, or at least remain as close to the forest as possible. He'd often talked with Ranger Brock about becoming a ranger himself and the ranger had never said a word to discourage him. And Noble, well, nobody worried too much about his plans, because they all knew that he'd be a success at whatever he decided to do with his life. But before they could really worry about such things, the pack still had to make it through high school. Considering their genetics and unique physical attributes, that was a task that was best tackled on a day-to-day basis.

Like today for example. Harlan had briefly stopped by his locker after entering the school, and then had quickly set off for his homeroom. In the past, he'd found that if he lingered chatting in the hallway, or by anyone else's locker chatting, some students would consider such loitering an invitation to tease and abuse him. Still, as careful as he was, that didn't mean he was safe.

"There he is," said a voice behind him.

Harlan didn't turn around to see who'd identified him, because he already knew. There was only one person in all of Redstone Secondary who cared where Harlan Brock was at any time during the school day, and that person was Jake MacKinnon.

The name alone had Harlan feeling sick to his stomach.

Jake MacKinnon was a throwback to the days when high-school bullies were a dime a dozen, and nobody gave them a second thought. These days there was plenty of talk about the problem of bullying, but not a lot of that talk managed to filter down into the hallways in the form of action. Or if it did, Jake MacKinnon wasn't listening. He'd been suspended from school twice by Principal Terashita, but being told to stay home from school wasn't much of a punishment for someone who was counting the days before he could quit school altogether and join a logging crew farther north. Knowing MacKinnon's luck, he'd probably be a foreman, terrorizing the workmen in his crew in less than five years. Either that or he'd be dead, killed in a bar fight or perhaps by one of his own crew in a logging "accident."

"Hold on a minute," MacKinnon said. "I just wanna talk, that's all."

Harlan felt the hairs on the back of his neck stand up on end. MacKinnon's talks usually drew a crowd, and taking a quick glance up and down the hall, this talk would be no different.

Jake MacKinnon began his harassment of Harlan in their first year of high school. Harlan had been on his way to math class when his books suddenly flew out from under his arms, thanks to a well-placed kick. Everyone had laughed at him. Harlan was tempted to tear Jake's throat out, but that very morning, Ranger Brock had warned the pack that they were not to use their wolfen powers on any of the students. So, instead of fighting, or even standing up to the bully, Harlan had simply picked up his books and moved on. MacKinnon had taken Harlan's passivity as a sign of fear, and he'd bullied him off and on ever since.

"Don'tcha want to talk to me?" MacKinnon said, moving his body in front of Harlan to block his way.

MacKinnon's shadow, a huge student named Del Zotto, giggled at MacKinnon's words.

"I've got nothing to say," Harlan said. That was true. He and MacKinnon had nothing in common other than both attending Redstone. They were rarely in the same class, had never shared a lunch period, and they rode to and from school on different buses. In fact, school aside, the two teenagers were exact opposites. Where Harlan was tall and lithe, MacKinnon was short and fat, weighing close to two hundred pounds. Harlan was quick and enjoyed playing games like badminton and table tennis, while MacKinnon had struggled to make the football team and had spent the last two years filling out a jersey on special teams. And where Harlan consistently had the top marks in all of his classes, MacKinnon rarely even attended them.

"That's bull," said MacKinnon.

Del Zotto snickered.

"I heard you in civics class today talking about the Charter of Rights." MacKinnon moved forward, pushing his face right up against Harlan's. "You were goin' on and on, blah-blah-blah . . . . I thought you were never going to shut up."

"Miss Thompson asked a question. Someone had to answer it."

Harlan was moving into dangerous territory. Miss Thompson hadn't just asked a question, she had asked MacKinnon the question. Then, after he'd hummed-and-ummed his way through a few lines about Life, Liberty and the pursuit of Happiness, she complimented MacKinnon on his knowledge of the American Declaration of Independence. When the laughter died down, she turned to Harlan and asked for the right answer.

"You were trying to make me look bad, weren'tcha?"

Harlan wanted to hold his tongue, but he'd had enough of MacKinnon and Del Zotto constantly grinning over his shoulder. "I wasn't trying to make you look bad," he said. "You were doing that all by yourself."

The crowd that MacKinnon had been so careful to gather around himself laughed, not with him, but at him.

"Nice one, Dogface!"

There it was, MacKinnon's trump card, the thing he kept in his back pocket for when all else failed.

Everyone was still laughing, but now it was at Harlan.

Harlan said nothing in response. What could he say? It was true, after all. While his siblings had all been blessed with attractive human faces, Harlan's face had retained many of his wolfen features, leaving him with a wide, puglike nose, an extended lower jaw that looked a bit like that of a bulldog, and large ears set high on his head that crested in a slight point. Some of the girls in his class thought Harlan was cute, but MacKinnon's "Dogface" line always got a laugh.

Edo van Belkom

"Asshole!" Harlan muttered, then turned to walk away.

"What did you say?" MacKinnon called out, grabbing Harlan's shoulder and spinning him back around.

Harlan said nothing, because nothing he said at this point would help. MacKinnon had come around looking to humiliate Harlan and he'd done it for the most part. All that was left was a few moments of taunting where MacKinnon would try to pick a fight, while Harlan did his best to ignore him.

"C'mon," prodded MacKinnon. "You're good with your mouth, are you any good with your fists?"

Harlan sighed. This was it, the real reason why MacKinnon picked on him. It was because he could. MacKinnon had figured out that no matter what he did, no matter how much he berated Harlan, taunted him, or insulted him, Harlan would never fight back. Not only that, no one would stick up for Harlan, either. Why should they? As long as MacKinnon picked on Harlan, then he wouldn't be picking on any of them. If anyone stood up for Harlan, they might become Jake's next target and no one wanted that. High school was difficult enough to get through without the likes of Jake MacKinnon on your case every day. Better to sacrifice one – in this case Harlan – for the greater good. It was a lousy thing to do, but it worked in its own perverse way.

"I'm not going to fight you," Harlan said.

"Not? Won't? Or can't?" MacKinnon spat. Then, just because he could, he added, "Dogface!"

16

Harlan shook his head and said, "Not." He could feel talons of rage tear at his insides. If he'd allowed himself, he could have changed form, torn apart this sack of fat standing in front of him, and chewed on his bones. But he couldn't because of a promise he'd made to Ranger Brock – a man to whom he and the other members of the pack owed their lives.

Just then MacKinnon lunged forward. The first time he'd done it, Harlan had jumped back and put his hands up to defend himself, which MacKinnon took to be a sign of fear. The second time, and every other time after that, Harlan remained still, doing his best to look bored while he wrestled against his emotions to keep himself from killing the stupid human in front of him. This time though, instead of lunging forward all the way, MacKinnon stopped, looked up, and retreated.

Harlan wondered if some breakthrough had been made. Perhaps the worst was over.

MacKinnon hitched the waistband of his pants slightly. "Need your big brother to fight your battles for ya?"

"What?" Harlan said. He turned around and saw that Argus had moved in behind him.

"Did I interrupt something?" Argus asked.

"Just Dogface, here, being chicken!"

Argus took a step forward.

"All right, all right," said another voice. Harlan glanced past his brother and saw Principal Terashita coming down the hall. "I hope you two weren't fighting."

MacKinnon smiled. "No, Sir. Fighting's against the rules. We were just talking."

Principal Terashita looked unconvinced. "Well, if you insist on more 'talking' I'm going to start taking people to my office."

Everyone knew it was a toothless threat, but it did the trick, sending MacKinnon on his way, and convincing the onlookers that the show was over. In moments the crowd was all but gone, leaving Harlan and Argus standing alone.

"You okay?" Argus asked, his voice edged with concern.

"Don't ever do that again!"

"What?"

"I don't need your help," Harlan said. "I don't need you to come to my rescue."

"But, I wasn't –"

"I can handle guys like MacKinnon myself."

Argus was about to say something in response, but Harlan turned his back on him and walked away.

"Hey, c'mon," Argus pleaded. "I was just trying to –"

But Harlan kept going. He knew it was wrong, but he was so angry he didn't know what else to do.

"Harlan isn't too happy with me," Argus said as he slid into a seat next to Noble at their usual table closest to the door in the cafeteria.

"I heard."

"You did?" Argus asked in surprise. "But how could you –"

"A couple of guys told me about Harlan's run-in with MacKinnon. They said you showed up at the end and scared MacKinnon off. I'm guessing Harlan didn't appreciate the help."

"No, he didn't," Argus said, unwrapping a ham and cheese sandwich and making half of it disappear with a single bite. "But I didn't do anything to that weasel MacKinnon, didn't even say anything to him," Argus said around a mouthful of sandwich. "I know Harlan wants to fight his own battles, but how can he expect me to stand by and do nothing when he's being pushed around by a human?" When Argus said the last word he leaned in close to Noble and whispered it like it was a secret word that no one else would understand.

Noble shrugged and took a sip from his milk carton. "There are things we could do to MacKinnon."

"Like what?"

"We could arrange to have someone give him a nuclear wedgie. You know, the kind where the underwear gets pulled up around the guy's ears."

Argus snickered. That would be nice. Wedgies like that hurt like hell, and there was no graceful way to pull the underwear out of your crack. Half the fun was watching someone trying to set themselves right. But as much as Argus wanted MacKinnon to get his, he knew it would never work. The smile lingered on Argus's face for a moment. When it was gone he turned to Noble and said, "But that would only make MacKinnon more angry at the world, and he'd end up taking it out on Harlan anyway."

Noble nodded. "And if word ever got around to Harlan that we'd arranged it, he'd never forgive us."

That was true. While there were plenty of guys who would be willing to give MacKinnon a wedgie or stuff one of their socks in his mouth or tape him to his locker, none of them could be trusted to keep quiet about doing Noble such a favor. They'd be too proud of themselves and would just have to brag. Or if they were hauled into the office, they'd tell Principal Terashita it was Noble's idea before the door even closed behind them. So, while the thought of a wedgie had been good for a laugh, it wasn't much help to Harlan.

Argus sighed. "But we just can't let MacKinnon pick on Harlan like that. If *I* find it embarrassing, imagine what it's doing to Harlan." Argus could feel the rage creeping into his muscles, along his arms, across his chest, and down his back. He took a deep breath and the feeling lessened, but didn't go away completely. "We've got to do something to stop it." A pause. "Before something bad happens . . . to MacKinnon."

Noble nodded once more. He knew just as well as Argus that Harlan would be able to put up with only so much, before he would fight back. When that happened, Jake MacKinnon would no longer be a problem, but there would be a whole set of new problems to take his place.

"I know we've got to stop it," Noble said, finishing off his milk in a gulp, "but I don't know how. At least not yet."

Chapter 3

It was two in the afternoon, and Donna Hughson had almost finished her walk around the north shore of Puntzi Lake. She went out every afternoon with her dog, a black lab named Daisy, that was never far from her side. She'd been living in a cabin just north of Redstone for six years now, having moved there after the death of her husband, John, to pursue her lifelong dream of becoming an artist. When she first moved into the cabin, the people around Redstone considered her to be a bit of a joke; just another rich old city woman wanting to get back to nature or "find herself" in the woods. But the old woman surprised everyone. She stuck it out, put in her own indoor plumbing, and hooked up a generator so she could paint after sundown.

When she first began to show her paintings, no one in town thought much of them. Sure, she could render a flower fairly well, and paint a deer or bobcat so you would know that's what you were looking at, but it was what she did with her subjects that eventually made people take notice.

Her *Wildflower* paintings usually featured an array of blossoms full of color and life, with one of them being unceremoniously trampled beneath a hiking boot. Then there were the *Forest* paintings, which featured stumps of huge trees just a few inches tall, with a sawdust-covered seedling struggling for life in their shadows. There were Hughson paintings hanging in the National Gallery of Canada and eight of the country's provincial art galleries. Her work had even been shown beside the paintings of several members of the Group of Seven at the McMichael Gallery.

Donna Hughson's walks with Daisy were always quiet outings. They both knew that a sound from either of them could scare off an animal or disturb a scene that might make for an excellent painting somewhere down the road.

That's why when Daisy began to bark, Donna knew something was very, very wrong.

"What is it, girl?" she asked.

Daisy barked and did a sort of half-leap in the air, rising up on her hind legs like a puppy might do to get at a ball held in its master's hand. But Daisy was no puppy, and there was nothing in Donna's hand. There was however, an unusual sound coming from somewhere off in the distance – a low rumble that was growing louder with each passing second.

Donna moved to the side of the road and turned in the direction of the sound. Daisy continued to bark and her leaps became more frenzied.

"Daisy!" Donna called in a commanding voice.

The dog kept on barking as she moved to Donna's side.

Donna squinted her eyes, then put a hand over them to shield them from the sun. She couldn't see anything other than an odd dark cloud rising up over the road. Her first thought was of smoke, except if the forest was on fire, the smoke would be over the trees, not the road. Perhaps it was a swarm of black flies, or mosquitoes. She'd never seen such a cloud of insects before, but she'd heard others swear they had.

And then all at once the mystery was solved as a bright red Peterbilt crested a rise in the roadway. Its chromed front end gleamed in the sunlight and its bright twin exhausts belched out a fresh cloud of blackish smoke that hung in the air between the trees on either side of the road.

"Get back, Daisy!" Donna said, grabbing the dog by her collar and moving them both off the road.

The red Peterbilt was followed by another and another, all connected to trailers loaded with tractors and machinery. Then came straight trucks and cube vans, and pickup trucks pulling bullet-shaped airstream trailers. The procession was a dozen vehicles long, each one of them displaying the Conservco Resources logo on all their doors. Then, just as the line of trucks was all but gone, a lone school bus, painted green and loaded with men, chugged past as if it were desperately trying not to be left behind.

Daisy barked the entire time the trucks rumbled past, and kept barking long after they'd gone.

"What are *they* doing here?" Donna wondered aloud. While there had been sections of the Redstone forest that had been slated for selective cutting, the road they were on didn't lead to any of the approved areas.

"Something's not right here."

Daisy barked in agreement.

"C'mon girl," Donna said, turning for home and moving as quickly as her aged bones would allow. "I think the police, or that ranger fellow . . . . What's his name again? Brock, that's it. I'm sure he'll want to hear about this."

Harlan walked down the main hallway on his way to his locker. His morning classes were done and he was carrying both his math and science textbooks against his right hip.

"Hi Harlan," a couple of cute girls said as he passed their locker.

"Oh, uh, hi girls," he responded, wondering why these two girls, these two good-looking girls, would want to say hello to him. That sort of stuff happened to Noble, sometimes even Argus, but never himself.

"Would you be able to help us with our science homework after lunch?" the blonde one asked. He'd seen her around the school and remembered her name was

Margaret, but all her friends called her Maggie. She was a bad girl who wore too much makeup, liked bad boys, and was always on the wrong side of right. But Harlan was able to overlook all that because she was hot, a real fox, and hey . . . she'd said hello to him.

"Sure, I could help you with your homework," he said, stopping next to her locker and casually leaning against it, like it was the most natural thing in the world. "In fact, I'd be happy to."

Maggie and her friend giggled.

And suddenly, Harlan felt sick to his stomach. Something was definitely not right here.

A moment later the books by his side were gone, kicked out of his hand by a big black boot. His books opened up as they spun through the air, their pages flapping like useless wings that did nothing to stop the books from landing on the floor with a loud *thwap*, and skidding to a stop.

Maggie and her friend howled with laughter.

And so did everyone else.

Harlan could feel the rage boil within him. He looked up and down for Jake MacKinnon and saw him waving from the far end of the hall. MacKinnon stood there a moment, then ducked into the library and out of sight.

Harlan picked up his books and began striding down the corridor intent on tearing Jake MacKinnon to pieces.

Suddenly a hand grasped his shoulder, slowing him down. He took two more steps before a second hand grabbed his arm.

"Don't," said Noble, tightening his grip on Harlan's shoulder.

"I want to hurt him," Harlan seethed. "Bad."

"We all do," said Argus, keeping a firm grip on Harlan's arm.

"You'll get your chance," Noble promised. "Just not now."

Chapter 4

Ranger Brock pulled to a stop on the side of the dirt road directly behind Sergeant Martin's cruiser. There were two other vehicles besides the ranger's 4 × 4, the first belonging to one of Sergeant Martin's constables, and the other, a minivan driven by the naturalist and artist, Donna Hughson. The sergeant had tried to tell the old woman to stay home and let the authorities handle the situation. But she'd been skeptical, citing their inability to stop that crackpot TV scientist, Doctor Edward Monk, from trying to steal a wolf from the forest several months earlier.

Ranger Brock liked Donna and had even bought one of her paintings for a wall in his living room at home. While the sergeant had been concerned that the old woman might get in the way, or maybe even hinder their efforts to find out what was going on, Ranger Brock was glad she'd tagged along. First of all, there was no one feistier than Donna when it came to preserving the forest, and having a civilian watch over the meeting between the police and the forestry company might help keep things from getting out of hand.

Ranger Brock turned off his engine and got out of his 4×4. Their little convoy had kicked up a fair amount of dust and the Conservco site supervisor was already out on the road ready to meet with them, along with a dozen or more of his biggest lumbermen.

"This should be fun," Sergeant Martin said as the ranger caught up to him.

"Maybe," said Ranger Brock. "But I think they'll need at least six more men to make it an even fight."

The sergeant smiled, greeted his constable, a young man named Neavis, and together the three of them headed for the wall of lumbermen lined up across the road.

"They're not supposed to be here," Donna Hughson said, bringing up the rear, several paces behind the two men.

Without warning, Sergeant Martin turned on his heels and put up his hand. "Look Donna, I appreciate getting your call, but you asked us to handle the situation, so let us handle it. I don't want to hear anything more from you."

She looked hurt. When she opened her mouth to speak, Sergeant Martin cut her off with an admonishing finger. "Or I'll have Constable Neavis, here, escort you back to your car. Understand?"

At last she nodded.

Satisfied, the sergeant turned back around and continued walking. "Do you know what you're going to say to him?"

Ranger Brock shook his head. He was familiar with most of the logging company employees who worked the redwood forest, but he'd never seen this man before. He was tall and lean and had a dark complexion, a mix of light and shadow with eyes that could hide a thousand little secrets and a half-dozen big ones. In a nutshell, he looked like he was from somewhere else. The ranger didn't like that one bit. He preferred to deal with people who were born and raised in the area; who had roots in the land and were aware that anything they did affected family and friends. This guy probably had ties to the company he worked for and that was about it. If things went bad, he'd be on the road back to wherever he came from in a minute, leaving the likes of Sergeant Martin and himself to clean up the mess.

"Afternoon," the sergeant said, tipping his cap slightly. "I'm Sergeant Martin, RCMP." He turned to his left, then right. "This is Constable Neavis, and Ranger Brock." He didn't bother to mention Donna, who looked on from behind.

"Gentlemen," the man said.

"You have a name?" asked Sergeant Martin.

He nodded and said, "Tyler Allen Ceballo."

No one in this part of the province went by three names, let alone two first ones. "You're from the city, aren't you?" asked Ranger Brock.

"West Vancouver," Ceballo said.

That figured. West Vancouver was a tony suburb where only the richest people could afford to live. The ranger had passed through the neighborhood once on his way to a conference and when he'd wondered aloud how anyone could afford to live in those houses, his colleague riding with him in the van said, "They screw the poor, how else?" This man looked capable of screwing the poor – and anyone else he could – just to get ahead.

"I'm a vice president of Conservco and this site's supervisor." He extended his hand. "My friends call me Ty."

Neither Sergeant Martin nor the ranger extended their hands. "This isn't a social call," the ranger said.

"Why? Is there a problem?" Ceballo asked, his smile growing wider. Ranger Brock saw that smile and disliked the man immediately. He could almost picture it on Ceballo's face as he plunged a knife into some animal's belly, or even deep into the back of one of his co-workers. The smile was menacing, maybe a bit evil, and it was a perfect match for the dark glint in the man's eyes. He was sure that this guy, this Tyler Allen Ceballo, was the type who would do just about anything to ensure he always came out on top.

"You're in the wrong place," Ranger Brock said.

Ceballo shook his head, and his smile lingered. "I don't think so . . . At least not according to the survey."

Ranger Brock could feel the hairs bristle on the back of his neck. "We just finished the survey. There's no way the chief forester has made a decision on any of the logging rights yet."

Ceballo shrugged. "When you get this deep into the forest, all the trees begin to look the same. That's why we've got our own people looking at the survey. You know, to help the chief forester come to the *right* decision."

Ranger Brock didn't like the sound of that at all. Obviously they were going to try and influence the chief forester and persuade him to allow Conservco to harvest the forests just north of Redstone. These were all old growth forests that had stood for hundreds of years. And while there were plenty of harvestable forests farther north of the town, they'd set up their camp here, because there was already a road in place that led to the site. If they began a couple of miles north on the other side of the river where logging operations had been discussed for the past twenty years, the company would have to build a new road to get there, or use helicopters to take the trees off the side of the mountain. Either way would dramatically increase the cost of each log, so there was a lot to be gained by staking an early claim to the land and the road that led to it.

Ranger Brock stepped forward. "You've got no right to this forest. Seems to me you're just making some kind of land grab."

Again the man smiled and shook his head, causing the ranger to like him even less. "I'm just following orders," he said. "But I suspect what you're saying might be true of the lawyers employed by my company. I believe there were an even dozen of them at last count, all working very hard with the chief forester's office to make sure everything's in order. In the meantime, we'll be providing additional information on things like fish habitats, soil, water . . . as well as the great economic benefits harvesting here will bring to the people of Redstone."

"Yeah, for a year, maybe two, then what?" The ranger felt the rage welling up inside him. This man was the kind who would clear out the forest until there wasn't a single tree left standing. And he'd do it all with that stupid smile on his face.

Sergeant Martin put a hand on Garrett's shoulder and took a step forward. "You can't start cutting yet," he stated.

"Not a branch," added Ranger Brock.

"Of course not, but there's no harm in getting ready . . . is there?"

Sergeant Martin said nothing. His lips pressed into a thin white line and he stared at the trees across the road in search of something to say. "Let's go," he said at last, his voice heavy with disappointment.

Ranger Brock sighed, and with the sergeant, headed back to their vehicles.

"What?" cried Donna. "That's it! You're just going to let them stay here?"

"They haven't broken any laws," the sergeant said.

That was true, thought Ranger Brock. And they probably wouldn't break any future laws either. It would be left to their lawyers in Victoria, who would bend as many rules as they could in order to convince the chief forester's office that their version of the survey was the correct one.

"But you can't just leave them here." The expression on the old woman's face was one of panic.

Ranger Brock was going to reassure Donna when Sergeant Martin stepped in front of her and said, "What would you like me to do? Draw my weapon and shoot them if they don't move their vehicles?"

Donna said nothing as the realization of how complicated the situation was sank in.

Yet, Garrett understood her predicament. If they started cutting here, the peace she'd enjoyed these past few years would be replaced by the constant whine of chainsaws and the rumble of logging trucks rolling past her cabin. "There's nothing more we can do right now," he said softly. "At least not until we get the results of the survey, and the chief forester has done all the technical analysis on the area."

Donna sighed in disgust.

Garrett felt sorry for the old woman. He even felt a little sorry for the lumbermen, who didn't quite know who they were dealing with here.

"Donna," he said. "You know a big part of any decision made by the chief forester is public comment. Even the forestry companies must consult the public and consider *all* forest values before they begin any activity. So, if you don't like what they're proposing, you've got the right to say your piece as loudly and as forcefully as you please."

"You mean, like a protest?"

"It worked in Clayoquot Sound."

Donna took a moment to consider it.

Clayoquot Sound had been slated for clear-cutting until public outcry and international protest got the area on the west coast of Vancouver Island designated an international biosphere by the United Nations Educational Scientific Cultural Organization. The move had preserved a vast area as a biosphere reserve. The same was unlikely to happen to Redstone, but there was still a good chance that any move made by Conservco could be blocked if enough people stood up and voiced their opinions.

"Maybe you're right," she harrumphed, then turned back to face the lumbermen. "You won't get away with this!" she shouted. "*I* won't let you."

The lumbermen all laughed at the old woman.

Garrett smiled too, but not for the same reason. Donna Hughson might look old and frail, but if there was going to be a fight, she was someone you wanted on your side.

An hour later Donna Hughson was making another long-distance phone call. She'd already called the papers in Prince Rupert, Prince George, and all of the other local dailies and weeklies she could think of. From Dawson Creek to Victoria, every media outlet in British Columbia was aware that something "not right" was going on in their little corner of the province.

Now that the alarm bell had been sounded, it was time for her to call out the big guns. Sure the newspapers and radio and television stations would all do a fine job of reporting the news to the rest of the country, but this was a fight that needed an army, and she knew just where to find one.

She dialed the ten-digit number.

Alise Grant was a sculptress in Toronto who did strange things with copper and clay. Her twisted renditions of people, places, and things were so abstract that no two people saw the same thing when looking at one of her works. But while critics and regular folk didn't always know what to make of her works, no fewer than fourteen of them were on exhibit in the Art Gallery of Ontario. But more than talented, Alise was a great organizer of people. She had friends in high places, low places, and all the places in between. If Donna needed an army, Alise was the general who could fill its ranks.

The phone rang twice.

"Hello?"

"Alise, this is Donna."

"Donna dear, how are you?"

"No time to talk now. We've got a problem here."

"What's wrong?"

"Have you got the list of writers' unions handy?"

"I think so."

"How about all the artists' guilds?"

"Yes."

"And that Canadian poets group?"

"Uh-huh."

"And Greenpeace . . . They'll want to know about this too, of course." At last she stopped a moment to take a breath.

"For God's sake Donna, what is it?"

"The logging trucks rolled into my forest today," she said. "And it's going to take every tree-hugging salad-eater you know to help get rid of them."

Chapter 5

Phyllis Brock put the last of the dinner plates on the table as Garrett spooned the chili out of the large pot on the stove.

"Are those men going to camp on the road tonight?" she asked.

"Some of them," Garrett said. "The rest will be back in the morning."

"What are they trying to prove?"

Garrett sighed. "I think they feel they'll have a better chance if they make an early claim and stay put. People will get used to them being here and when it comes time to make an assessment on the land, people won't care one way or another what happens."

"Surely they won't get away with this."

"You'd think that, wouldn't you?" Garrett said, spooning out the last of the chili and handing the bowl to his wife. "But the ministry lawyers I talked to today aren't so sure. They think the company might have put together a good case for harvesting close to town."

"A good case!"

"They say it will all come down to public reaction, and the company has a way of swaying public opinion with talk of jobs and prosperity."

At that moment, Noble stepped into the dining room, followed closely by his brothers and sister. "What's going on?"

"Why don't you sit down first?" said Garrett.

"Something serious?" Argus asked.

"Sit down," the ranger repeated. "We can talk while we eat."

The four took their seats around the table. Phyllis and Garrett joined them.

"Well, what is it?"

The ranger took a deep breath and began. "A logging crew from Conservco rolled into the forest near Puntzi Lake this morning."

At the mention of Puntzi Lake, Argus stopped eating and directed all of his attention to what the ranger was saying.

"They want to harvest the forest on the south side of the river, which will give them full access to the road."

Harlan shook his head. "I didn't know the road was part

of the survey. Sounds like they're trying to grab more land and save money by taking the road."

The ranger put his spoon in his bowl of chili and left it there. "That's what it looks like."

"They can't do that!" Tora said, looking around the table. "Can they?"

All eyes, including Tora's, shifted toward the end of the table where Ranger Brock sat. His head was down and he was looking at his chili as if the answer to the question was lying somewhere at the bottom of the bowl. "The truth is . . . there isn't any real reason why they *can't* harvest the forest here. There's no endangered species in the area, no tourism or recreational value to speak of. The only reason why they shouldn't harvest here is the site is too close to the town, and there are plenty of people around here who don't see that as much of a problem at all. And the longer they're camped out there, people will see it as less and less of a problem." The ranger's voice sounded tired, like he'd just been through one of the longest days of his life. "The decision is ultimately up to the chief forester, but since they're also trying to fudge the survey results, anything can happen."

No one said a word for several moments.

Finally, he added, "Someone even told me that if they get the go-ahead to harvest, Conservco will be pushing for a clear-cut instead of thinning select trees."

Argus banged a fist on the table, making the plates and cutlery clang like an alarm bell. "They must be stopped!"

"Of course they must," said the ranger in a calm, yet forceful voice. "And they will be. It's just not going to happen overnight." Another sigh. "It'll take time for all the information to be analyzed by the authorities. Conservco's has made the first strike, but there'll be plenty of protesters to help shape public opinion – Donna Hughson will make sure of that. With any luck, it'll be enough to convince the company that this bit of land's not worth the trouble."

"And if it isn't?" Argus asked.

The ranger didn't answer.

"There has to be some reason why they can't harvest here," offered Tora.

The ranger smiled. "I'm sure there is, but no one knows what it is yet."

Argus hadn't moved since he'd asked his question. Finally he said, "I know why."

"Why?" the ranger asked.

Argus said nothing for several seconds as if searching for the right words, then he began. "This morning on our run through the forest I saw something on the trail – something different."

"Yeah, I was in the lead," Harlan said, smartly.

Argus ignored Harlan's comment. "I don't know what it was. I've never seen anything like it before. It looked like a big, hairy man, but even though I only saw it for a moment, I could tell it was magical somehow. More than a man, it was a powerful being at one with the forest." He stopped to take a breath. "It lives there among the animals. The forest is its home. The trees there can't be cut down."

Tora looked from Argus to Ranger Brock. "It sounds like he saw a Bigfoot."

Harlan laughed. "A Sasquatch? And me without my camera." Harlan flinched, expecting Argus to give him a playful push or punch in the arm. Instead, Argus remained motionless, and it was Noble that gave Harlan a punch for being so insensitive to his bigger brother's vision.

Garrett said nothing for the longest time, thinking of just the right way to address the situation. At last he spoke. "I'm sure Argus saw *something*, and it's possible that whatever it is, we don't know about it. After all, there are all kinds of people who don't know about you four."

The smile was suddenly gone from Harlan's face.

"And if there is something in those woods, then that's all the more reason we've got to do everything we can to save them from the saw."

Argus gave a slight nod and resumed eating his chili.

Noble, however, sat motionless, staring blankly at the ceiling as the seeds of a plan began to take root in his mind.

Chapter 6

After school the next day, Noble purposely missed the bus and walked into downtown Redstone, instead. He'd given a lot of thought to the problem of Conservco setting up shop in the forests around Puntzi Lake, and had been able to refine his plan during geography class that afternoon.

Logging rights weren't granted without public consent and it was really up to the people of Redstone to decide where and how much they allowed the logging companies to harvest. To Noble and the pack's way of thinking, the forests were a national treasure and should never, under any circumstances, be cut down. That's what he felt in his heart, but it wasn't a simple matter of black and white. Sure, the forests held a special place in all their hearts, and

Ranger Brock had similar feelings of his own for the land. But they were living in the middle of British Columbia where a great many people made their living either by working in the forestry industry, or providing services to the people who did. For that reason, you couldn't just send logging companies packing every time one of them wanted to cut down some trees. People needed to work and make a living, and there were still plenty of forests to harvest. The real question wasn't how much or when, but where.

As far as Noble understood the problem, Conservco had the inside track on harvesting the forests north of Puntzi Lake. The trouble was that the company had staked out an area that was more generous than the survey allowed. They did it in order to incorporate the existing road networks, thereby making the harvest more profitable than if they had to build their own inroads. The situation seemed pretty straightforward and would probably resolve itself before long, but Noble had learned his lesson about such things when Tora had been kidnapped. He had trusted then that the government would protect his sister and keep her from being taken out of the forest. But that hadn't happened and they'd had to rescue her from a madman themselves.

This time, Noble was going to do something before it was too late, and that something involved Willie Greene. Willie was the unofficial town character, and made a living doing odd jobs and taking small acting roles in television and movie productions whenever they were in the area. Willie wasn't an especially talented actor. One of his more prominent roles had been "Native Number Two" in an episode of the *X-Files*. He was also a model. Every couple of months a camera crew would roll into town to shoot Willie's picture for use in ads for one sort of herbal medicine or another.

When he reached town, Noble went straight to the Petro-Canada station on Main Street, knowing that Willie often spent his afternoons there chatting with the day cashier, Arlo Mundt.

"Noble Brock," Arlo said, when Noble stepped into the office. "What brings you here?" He craned his neck to look at the pumps. "Not a car, I see."

"I'm looking for Willie Greene."

"Your father got some work for him?"

Noble thought about it. Willie sometimes worked on fire crews organized by Ranger Brock, or else manned watch-towers on a part-time casual basis during fire season. The work seemed to suit Willie, especially the casual part. Noble needed Willie for a job, but it wasn't exactly what you would call work. "Not really," Noble answered. "I need to see him."

"Try the library," said Arlo. "He said he needed to check on his fortune . . . you know, to see if he was gonna eat steak or Kraft Dinner tonight." Arlo laughed at that, but Noble didn't join him. There was nothing funny about being poor in Redstone, especially during the winter months.

"Thanks," Noble said, leaving the office and heading for the library around the corner.

The Redstone Public Library was a fairly new building, made of brick and mortar, but faced with cut cedar logs to give it an old-style log cabin look. Noble found Willie, not at a desk in the stacks, but at a computer station, surfing the Internet.

"Willie Greene?" he said.

"Who wants to know?" Willie asked without taking his eyes off the screen. He wore a small pair of granny glasses low down on his nose that made his whole head tilt backwards when he looked at the monitor. As far as Noble could tell, Willie was checking out some sort of investments page. The name in the top right-hand corner of the screen read Willie Greene, and some of the figures on the page had as many as six digits. Maybe that's why Arlo was laughing, Noble thought. Willie wasn't poor at all, he just lived his life as if he were.

"I do," said Noble. "Noble Brock."

"One of Ranger Brock's kids?" Willie finally turned to look at Noble, and smiled. "Oh yeah, you're the good-looking one."

Noble felt his face getting warm. He'd been called the "good-looking one" plenty of times before, but he'd never liked it since the people who called him that also usually referred to Harlan as "the runt" or "Dogface."

"I need you to do something," Noble said.

Willie glanced at Noble a moment, then began looking around the library as if he expected to find a camera hidden somewhere between the books.

"Your father send you?"

"Nope, I came on my own."

Willie must have been intrigued, because he closed the file on the screen and turned to face Noble. "Okay, I'll bite. What is it?"

All at once Noble understood why Willie sometimes got work as a model. He was only in his mid-to-late thirties, forty at the most, but his face was etched with lines that seemed to be carved by time's own knife. There was character in his features, suggesting a hard, but proud life. There was also something distinguished, perhaps even handsome, about his features. Noble adjusted himself in his seat and began to explain. "Yesterday a crew from Conservco set up camp near Puntzi Lake."

"I heard."

"Well, they're trying to claim the road leading into the site and that's not right."

"It'll mean jobs for a lot of people around here."

"The jobs will be there even if they move north. There'll be more of them in fact, since they'll have to build new roads to gain access to the forests." Noble paused a moment, not wanting to waste any more time arguing right and wrong. "They're setting up too close to town and you know it."

"Okay, so you want them gone. What do you want me to do, tell them to get lost?"

"Sort of."

Willie shook his head. "You seem to be confusing me with some Mohawk warrior you read about in *Maclean's*. I'm an actor, not a fighter."

"I know, that's why you're perfect for the job."

"Job? You want me to work for you?" Willie chuckled softly under his breath. "I'm an ACTRA member, you know. I get union scale."

Noble shook his head. "I don't have money to pay you."

"Then why should I do it?"

Noble gave that some thought. "Do you do everything you do for money? What about community service?"

"Sorry kid, but I don't work for free . . . It's the principle of the thing."

Noble's shoulders slumped and he let out a sigh.

Willie must have noticed the change in Noble's attitude because he suddenly began trying to do damage control. "Look, I'd help you if I could, but I'm a busy man. I've got all kinds of irons in the fire. I never know which one's going to get hot, so I've got to keep myself available in case some real work comes in."

Noble nodded, then said, "Aren't you even interested in what I want you to do?"

Noble must have said the right thing because Willie's expression suddenly changed. He gave Noble a half-smile, shrugged and said, "Doesn't cost anything to listen. Go ahead . . . make your pitch."

Noble took a deep breath, then began. "It's a standoff up there, and in another day or two there'll be protesters and demonstrations. Once that gets going there'll be plenty of media – newspaper, radio, and television people from all across the country, maybe even around the world."

Willie said nothing at first, but Noble could tell from the expression on the man's face that he was growing more and more interested. "And where do I fit in?"

"You'll basically be playing yourself, but instead of being an actor, you'll be playing someone who is at one with the forest. You'll get in front of the cameras and tell millions of people all over the world how this part of the forest is sacred to your people and cannot be disturbed. There are spirits who live in the forest and their home must be preserved."

Willie was silent, looking pensively at a far corner of the library's ceiling. A wider, fuller smile slowly broke over his face. "I like it, kid, except there's just one problem. I'm Haida. My tribe lives on the coast."

Noble shrugged. "That's just a small detail. If they ask you about your heritage, you can tell them whatever you like, but I'm betting most of the journalists that come up here won't know or even think about it once they hear your story."

Willie seemed to consider that. "You really think they'll be coming here from all over the world?"

"I can't say for sure, but I can tell you that Donna Hughson is organizing the protesters."

"That old bag!" Willie exclaimed in a fond, almost admiring tone.

Noble nodded. "She's already got a bunch of tree-huggers coming up from the city."

"Yeah, I bet she does . . ."

It looked as if Willie might do it. All that was needed was one last little nudge to push him over the top. "They'll fight the fight, and you'll be the symbol of their protest." Willie was almost there, but not quite. Noble decided it was now or never. "An icon, respected and revered the world over."

Silence, as Noble's words hung in the air like smoke.

"Good roles have been hard to come by lately." A pause. "Hard to come by, period."

"Then you'll do it?"

"Ah, why the hell not."

Chapter 7

By dinnertime, everyone in Redstone was talking about the standoff between the logging company and the conservationists that was going on in the forest north of the town. News of the situation had spread like wildfire and already people were lining up on one side or the other. As far as Noble and the others could tell, the two groups were pretty much split equally. The nature lovers, led by Donna Hughson, wanted to preserve as much of the forests as they could, especially those parts that were closer to town. Others supported the loggers because, after all, the town's lifeblood was the forestry industry. To chase away a logging company for whatever reason was just bad business. Of course, there were rumors that Tyler Allen Ceballo and his Conservco cronies had been freely spreading fifty- and hundred-dollar bills around Redstone to buy people's support – especially in Clancy's bar – but no one seemed willing, or able, to admit to taking the company's money just yet.

After they ate, the pack transformed into their wolfen forms and headed up to the camp to see for themselves what was going on.

When they arrived a half hour later, they took up a position behind a stand of trees where they could watch unnoticed from the road. The logging company equipment was parked in a crude semicircle, forming a wall between the roadway and the section of forest they were planning on clear-cutting. The loggers were all standing in front of their machines, arms crossed and watching the opposing sides clash in front of them.

On the right side of the road, a dozen or more pickup trucks were parked on the shoulder, with countless burly men – mainly lumberjacks, hoping to get hired on once the cutting started – milling about their trucks, chatting amongst themselves, smoking cigarettes, and every so often drinking Kootenay from a can. Whatever they were doing, they were doing it with an eye on the spectacle taking place across the road.

On the left side of the road, Donna Hughson, Daisy, and four friends had begun to make their stand. Overnight they'd constructed signs and placards that read: LEAF OUR FORESTS ALONE and REDSTONE IS NOT FOR SALE! They were now chanting and walking in front of the loggers in an endless circle.

"Please, please, save our trees!" they shouted in unison, with Daisy punctuating the chant with irregular barks.

And then, through the megaphone she usually used at the annual community center garage sale, Donna Hughson piped up, "No deforestation without public consultation!"

It was an odd sight, all those lumbermen standing around watching four tiny gray-haired ladies and a dog fighting the good fight.

Not much of a fight, but at least it was a start.

There were a few other people out on the road. Ranger Brock and Sergeant Martin were there, as well as John G. Smith, the reporter from the *Redstone Gazette*, the town's local weekly newspaper. A tall, thin man with curly hair, a bald spot, and a full beard, Smith was accompanied by a young woman with a tape recorder who was introducing herself to different people in order to interview them for some radio station or broadcast network.

She approached Sergeant Martin for a comment, but he declined, stepping back from her with his hands in the air like she was holding a gun to him instead of a microphone. She nodded, then moved on to Ranger Brock. He seemed uncomfortable at first, having had a bad experience with media types in the past – and one Doctor Edward Monk, in particular. But he warmed up to her, and in minutes they were talking freely. Noble wanted to get closer to listen to what the ranger was saying, but he risked being spotted and that was too much of a chance to take. Besides, he could easily ask the ranger about the interview later that night.

But then the ranger and the reporter stopped talking. In fact, everyone stopped what they were doing and turned to look south.

Walking up the road with slow, measured steps, was Willie Greene. He was wearing several feathers in his hair, and an odd assortment of clothing that was full of bright colors and jagged patterns, as if he'd survived an explosion in a paint factory. As Willie neared, Noble motioned to the pack that he was going to move in closer. Argus nodded in acknowledgment and the others made themselves comfortable behind the stand of trees.

Noble crept forward, careful not to allow himself to be seen. There was a good chance one or more of the loggers had shotguns in their trucks, and they wouldn't hesitate to use them against a wolf – especially one that wasn't afraid to get so close to humans.

By the time Willie reached the protesters, they'd all stopped their chanting and put down their signs. Everyone's attention, seemed to be focused on the odd man in the colorful costume. Noble took the opportunity to move even closer.

"Willie?" said Donna Hughson. "Have you come to help us?"

Willie didn't answer. Instead he walked right on past the protest toward the logging company camp and didn't stop until he was standing in front of the biggest tractor. "Who is in charge?" he asked. Noble had seen some of Willie's work on television before, but he'd never heard him speak with such a powerful and dramatic voice.

"Who wants to know?" countered one of the workers, but only after he'd blown a long plume of cigarette smoke in Willie's face.

"I do," said Willie.

"And you are?"

"People around here know me as Willie Greene," he said, his words sounding like they had been spoken by a man in his late sixties or early seventies. "But I am also the shaman for the people of these forests."

The logger let out a little laugh, then shook his head. "There are no *people* living in these woods."

"That *you* know of," answered Willie, his face stoic and unsmiling.

"Oh, we know all right," said a voice from behind one of the big machines. There was silence for a moment, then a man appeared who walked and acted as if he were in charge. He was tall and thin, with neatly pressed jeans and a long-sleeve shirt that didn't have a single stain on it. He was from the city, and Noble distrusted him immediately. "We know," he said. "We did a survey and found there isn't a soul living between here and fifty miles north."

"Humans may not live here, but others do."

"Oh yeah, like who?" The man was obviously playing along with Willie and the look on his face told Noble that he considered all of this – especially Willie and the protesters – to be one big joke.

"The wolf and the deer are my brothers. The bear, my cousin."

"Aw, gimme a break."

"The eagle and the hawk, my uncles."

The man chuckled. "Catch me having Christmas dinner at your house." The rest of the loggers all erupted in laughter.

Willie, to his credit, remained unmoved, his face stoic. "Their spirits are strong here," he said. "As are the spirits of those of my tribe who have been buried here."

That caught the man off guard for a moment. He turned his head to the side and looked at Willie through narrowed eyelids. "There are no burial grounds here . . . we checked."

"That *you* know of," Willie said, his voice sounding stronger as he went along. "I assure you, they are here and if you clear-cut this land, the spirits will be angry and bad things will happen to the white man."

The man wasn't laughing anymore, but there was still a suspicious look on his face. "Wait a minute!" he said, snapping his fingers. "I know you. I've seen you in town. You call yourself an actor, but everyone else in town calls you a bum."

Noble held his breath, waiting to see how Willie would respond. Again, Willie proved he was a true professional. He ignored the man's comment and continued to play his role without the slightest hint of a reaction. "That is but one of my names. I'm also known as . . . *Manchoka*, the veil between man and spirit."

"Right! And I'm Wayne Gretzky."

Willie bowed. "An honor to meet you, oh Great One."

Everyone laughed at that, loggers and protesters alike.

"We're done here," the man said, turning his back on Willie. "And it's going to take a lot more than cheap actors in clown suits to get us out of here, Willie whatever-your-name-is."

Willie's face remained unchanged. "A single drop of water can divide mountains . . . over time." And with that, Willie turned and began walking down the road in the direction he'd come from, his stride every bit as strong and dignified as when he'd arrived.

Noble sighed and shook his head. Willie's heart had been in the right place, but he'd looked ridiculous in that outfit. What he'd said had sounded so . . . well, stupid, that no one with a brain and a heartbeat was ever going to believe he was a shaman. Noble was going to have to come up with another plan.

But just then someone called out Willie's name.

"Willie!" the radio reporter shouted.

Willie kept walking.

"I mean, Manchoka!"

Willie stopped, slowly turned, and waited for the female reporter to catch up to him.

They exchanged a few words, and Willie nodded. The reporter switched on her tape recorder and held the microphone up to Willie's lips.

Noble looked on in amazement, leaning forward to get a better look. Either Willie was a better actor than Noble thought, or the radio reporter was in desperate need of a story. Whatever the reason, it looked like the plan just might work after all.

Without a sound, he backed away from the protest and rejoined the rest of the pack, each of them waiting and ready for the long run home.

Later that evening, Noble put on his coat and shoes and told Ranger Brock and Phyllis he was going for a walk. He was just about to leave the house when Argus came up behind him.

"Where you going?" Argus asked.

"For a walk."

"Where are you *really* going?"

Noble looked down the hall to check where Ranger Brock was, then whispered, "I need to speak to Willie Greene."

"Mind if I tag along?"

Noble shook his head and gestured down the hallway. "Not if you square it with them first."

"I'm going with Noble," Argus said.

"Stay out of trouble, you two," came the response from Ranger Brock.

Argus shook his head. The ranger probably suspected something was up, but he knew enough not to interfere.

"Will do," said Argus, as the two boys left the house.

They walked the road to town in silence for several minutes before Argus asked, "What do you want to talk to Willie for?"

"I want to make sure he's going to show up tomorrow."

Argus hesitated a moment, then said, "You *told* him to do that?"

Noble couldn't help but smile. "He didn't think of it by himself, that's for sure."

"What about that costume?"

Noble shook his head. "*That* was his idea."

"You think it'll work?"

A little laugh. "You got a better idea?"

They walked in silence again until Argus cleared his throat and said, "I want to talk to you about something."

Noble shrugged. "Go ahead. We've got time."

"Okay . . ." A pause. "Well, it's no secret I'm not doing all that well at school."

"It's a human school," Noble said. "It's got walls and windows and locks on the doors. It's not the best environment for someone like you."

Argus smiled, appreciating his brother's understanding. "Sometimes I don't know what I'm doing there."

"We all feel like that from time to time, but it's important that we graduate because we won't be able to do much in the human world without a high-school diploma."

Argus was quiet for the longest time. Finally he said, "I don't think I'm going to graduate."

"Of course you are. Harlan's been hacking into the school computer to make sure you're a straight *C* student."

"That's not what I mean," said Argus. He put a hand on his brother's shoulder and turned Noble around to face him. "I'm thinking of leaving the pack . . . living in the forest. I might even find another pack to run with."

Noble felt his heart drop. He'd been expecting something like this from Argus, but not for another year or two.

Argus was a fighter and, as such, he was constantly being frustrated by the limitations imposed on him by the human world. It was killing Argus to stand by and watch Harlan being bullied by Jake MacKinnon, when every instinct he had told Argus to tear the little jerk apart. "But you're part of *our* pack," Noble said. "We *need* you."

Argus nodded. "I know, but *I* need something else. I feel my future is out there –" He gestured toward the woods. "– and it's calling me. Into the forest and away from the pack."

Noble turned and resumed walking. It was obvious that his brother had given the matter a lot of thought. They were talking about what he felt in his heart, not some child's dream of becoming a fireman. "Have you told Ranger Brock?"

Argus took a deep breath. "Not yet. I've got to get my courage up first."

"You? Courage?"

"He's a great man. I don't want to hurt him . . . or Phyllis."

"He'll understand," said Noble. "Just like I do." A pause. "It's your life. You have to do what *you* want to do with it. I'll be sad, but I won't stand in your way."

"Thanks," Argus said, resting a hand on Noble's shoulder. "I appreciate it."

The two brothers continued on into town.

They caught up to Willie Greene behind the bowling alley. He was slumped over on the back stairs drinking something from a paper bag.

"Willie, what are you doing?" Noble asked, as the actor took another sip from the bag.

He shook his head and coughed. "I've had a cold for days now," he said. "Doctor gave me a prescription for this cough medicine." He pulled the tiny brown bottle from the bag. "I'm supposed to have a tablespoon of the stuff, but I didn't want to wait until I got home."

"Oh," Noble said.

Argus laughed.

"Why? What did you think I was doing?"

Noble kicked at a stone and sent it rolling down the laneway. "Well, I thought you might be depressed about how it went today and, you know . . ."

"Was drowning my sorrows with a bottle of whiskey?"

Noble could feel the blood rushing to his face. "Yeah, something like that."

Willie smiled and pocketed the bag of cough medicine. "You've been watching too much television. I might play that kind of character, but I haven't had a drink since I was a teenager. Probably about your age, as a matter of fact."

"I didn't know that."

"Of course you didn't. And that's because a lot of people in this town made up their minds long ago about who and what Willie Greene is . . . . Who cares what the truth is?"

"So what is the truth?" Argus wanted to know.

"The truth is . . . I'm not exactly what I seem, and I'll leave it at that."

Noble nodded in understanding. Willie wasn't the only one in the alley who had a secret life.

"Never mind all this," Willie said, getting up off the steps and heading out of the alley. "What are you two doing here?"

Noble looked at Argus, then back at Willie. "To be honest, I came down to make sure you'd be going back to the protest tomorrow . . . that you weren't too discouraged."

Willie's grin was ear to ear. "You think I've never had a bad opening night before? Sure, my dialogue needs work, and the costume could be toned down a bit, but I think I've got something here with this Manchoka character. I've already got one radio interview out of it, and that's one more than I expected."

"Manchoka," Noble repeated. "What does the name mean?"

"Beats me," Willie shrugged. "I made it up. Sounds pretty good, don't it?"

Noble smiled and nodded. Willie was more of a professional than Noble – or anyone else in town – had given him credit for. If Willie was determined to see this through to the end, then Noble and the pack would have to do everything in their power to help him.

"About your dialogue," Noble said. "Maybe Argus and I could take you over to the library and work on some new material for tomorrow."

"Hey, that would be great!"

"What do you say, Argus?"

Argus shrugged. "Libraries and I don't usually mix, but . . . it's for a good cause."

"That's the spirit."

Willie's face lit up. "Speaking of spirits, I had a few ideas for tomorrow . . ."

Willie kept talking all the way to the library.

Chapter 8

I t was printed on yellow paper, and when Tora caught
  sight of it everything else on the bulletin board seemed
to vanish.

DRAMA NIGHT AUDITIONS
AFTER SCHOOL NEXT MONDAY
IN THE AUDITORIUM

There were three short plays listed that Principal
Terashita wanted to put on this year. Each of the plays was
about twenty minutes long with four or five different roles.
That meant the chances were good that Tora could get a
lead role in at least one, as well as a smaller part in one of
the others. Principal Terashita had talked about the plays

he'd selected and the one Tora was most interested in was *Red Carnations*, a romantic play about a young man and woman troubled by a case of mistaken identity. In the end the two resolve their problems, realize they are in fact looking for each other, and best of all . . . the play ends with a romantic and heartfelt kiss.

"What's up?" said a voice behind Tora, as she lingered in front of the flyer, considering the possibilities.

"It's the auditions for the school play," she said, turning around to see Michael Martin standing behind her.

"I can see that," he said, putting a hand on her shoulder. "Have you decided which play you want to star in?"

Tora smiled at him. Michael Martin always seemed to know just the right thing to say. He was teasing her, but not making fun of her aspirations. After hearing about the upcoming auditions, she'd talked about nothing else for weeks, describing each play in detail and making suggestions about the casting of each role from the group of students who usually came out for the drama club.

"*Red Carnations*," she said.

"I thought so."

There was a crowd around the bulletin board now, as more students became aware that the audition notice had been posted.

"You think I'd do well in it?"

"You'd be good in any of the plays . . . but you'd be great in that one."

"You really think so?" Tora asked, fishing for a compliment.

"Yeah, I do."

Tora resisted the urge to grin. She really liked Michael Martin, and she knew he liked her, too. As a result, he was likely to say anything to make her happy. "Thanks. But you're just saying that."

Michael shook his head. "No I'm not. In fact, I was thinking about trying out for the male lead in *Red Carnations*, so I'd be able to act in it with you."

Tora's eyes widened and a great big smile spread across her face. "That would be so cool!" she said.

"You have to get the part first," said a female voice.

Suddenly, all the fun was over. Tora turned around and saw Maria Abruzzo standing there in the hallway with a devilish smirk on her face.

"Hello Maria," Tora said, saying the girl's name slowly so there could be no mistaking how Tora felt about her. Tora disliked Maria Abruzzo, plain and simple. Maria never missed an opportunity to make fun of Tora, especially in front of the other students. Her favorite thing was to point out to everyone how hairy Tora was. Tora, for her part, did her best to keep her legs and arms covered on problem days, but every once in a while a bit of extra hair would make it onto the top of her hands, her legs, her arms, or God forbid, her face. When that happened, Maria Abruzzo was always there to point it out. It was particularly frustrating for Tora because after herself, Maria was probably the hairiest girl in the school. But unlike Tora, Maria didn't have the excuse of being a lycanthrope going for her. Maria was just one hairy, hairy girl. And mean.

"Just to let you know, I'm going for the lead role in *Red Carnations*, too. So you may want to try for something else to avoid being disappointed. I think there's a part for a sheepdog in one of the other plays."

The rest of the students switched their attention away from the bulletin board and onto the two girls.

Tora could feel the anger rising within her. She balled her right hand into a fist to hide the talons that were forming at the ends of her fingers, then shook her head. "No, you misread that. The role doesn't call for a dog, it calls for a bitch . . . which I think would suit your talents much better."

"Ooooo . . ." said the crowd of students in unison.

Maria's lips came together in a tight line, and her eyes squinted half shut as she glared at Tora. She took a step forward.

Principal Terashita was suddenly there between them. "Now, now girls," he said. "It's an audition, not a competition, so let's tone it down a bit." When he had control over the situation he raised his head to address the rest of the students. "We just want to see what you can do. You might try out for one part, but get a different one instead. We're going to put people in the roles they'll do best in, so all the pieces are as good as we can make them." He lowered his head and looked at Tora and Maria. "Okay? Understand?"

The two girls nodded.

"Great," Principal Terashita said as he walked away. "See you after school."

The two girls stood there for the longest time before

Maria finally said. "Oh, I forgot to tell you. I'll be rehearsing with Brad Horton." She flashed Tora that same smirk as before. "Good luck."

Tora felt all the strength drain out of her body. Brad Horton was a pro. He'd won awards in all sorts of provincial drama competitions and he'd acted in several television shows shot in and around Redstone and Vancouver. He was the best actor in the school, and he was going to make Maria's performance that much better.

"Don't worry," said Michael. "She might be auditioning with Brad, but she'll still be Maria Abruzzo. Nothing's going to change that sad little fact."

A hint of a smile crept onto Tora's face. Then she looked at Michael and laughed. "Thanks."

"No problem."

"Come on," she said, taking him by the hand.

"Where are we going?"

"To the library. We've got to practice."

The pack had just stepped off the school bus and were on their way to the house when Ranger Brock pulled up in his 4 × 4.

"Willie Greene's holding a press conference in half an hour," he said through the open window. "I thought you guys might want to be there to hear what he has to say."

"We sure would," said Noble.

Harlan pumped a fist into the air. "Anything to put off math homework for a while."

"I'm with you on that," agreed Argus.

Tora said nothing. She was too busy reading lines from a book of plays to comment, but she followed her brothers into the ranger's vehicle.

"Are they expecting a lot of media there?" Harlan asked from the backseat as they got under way.

The ranger shrugged. "Willie said he'd been e-mailing newspapers and radio stations all day long. Not a lot of them got back to him, but he's thinking most reporters will just show up for the press conference."

"That doesn't sound very promising," said Argus.

Noble nodded. "We're a long way from anywhere with a decent-sized newspaper or radio station."

"That's true, but in this day and age, it only takes one reporter to get the word out," said Ranger Brock. "Besides, Donna Hughson is starting a website for the protest and she needs Willie's press conference to provide some content for it."

That made sense. In the era of the World Wide Web it was possible for a single digital camera to record the audio and video of an event, and once that footage was uploaded onto a website, any news outlet in the world would have access to it in order to use it in any way they wished.

"A website, huh?" said Harlan. "I guess she's not as old fashioned as she looks."

They reached the protest site twenty minutes later. There was a makeshift podium made out of a length of log stood on end by the side of the road. At least one reporter had placed a microphone on the podium and there were several people gathered around, most likely waiting for Willie's arrival. Donna Hughson and a few of her friends were handing out hot chocolate and biscuits. There were some takers, mostly loggers.

In the backseat Tora looked up from her book. "Where is everybody?"

"Maybe we're early," offered Argus.

"No," said Ranger Brock. "We're here on time. Willie's the one who's late."

They all got out of the 4×4 and headed over to the podium. A few minutes later, Willie Greene made the same walk down the road as he'd done the day before. His costume had been toned down quite a bit overnight, with most of the bright colors being exchanged for earth tones of green and brown with just a few accents of aquamarine. He was also sporting more feathers. And even though such adornments weren't customary for Native Canadians in this part of the country, they made Willie look a bit more like people would expect him to look.

Willie stepped up to the podium and thanked everyone for coming.

Noble expected there would be movement around the podium as the reporters closed in to hear what Willie had to say, but nothing happened. The only media people there were John G. Smith from the *Gazette* and the same female radio reporter Willie had spoken to the day before.

"These men," Willie said, referring to the people from Conservco, "are here because they want to harvest the

Earth Mother's bounty from these lands. We, the people of the First Nations, don't oppose such things. After all, the Earth Mother wouldn't provide us with such a gift if she did not intend for us to accept and make use of it."

Argus gave Noble a nudge with his arm. "It sounds a lot better now than it did last night."

Noble smiled. They had spent close to two hours in the library putting together Willie's speech. It did sound a lot better today, but that was probably because Willie had spent all day rehearsing his lines. Too bad there weren't a lot of people around to hear it.

"Indeed, we have harvested her bounty in the past, and we will continue enjoying the benefits of her gifts, but only with the utmost respect for her generosity. The Earth Mother is powerful, and to exhibit greed in her presence for her gifts will only make her angry."

Ranger Brock turned to Noble with a curious look on his face. He leaned in closer to Noble and said, "Is this the same Willie who was here yesterday?"

Noble shrugged.

Donna Hughson must have overheard the ranger because she said, "He is good, isn't he?"

"It is common sense," Willie continued. "Even the government of British Columbia recognizes that and has designated nearly twenty-nine million acres of protected lands where no forestry, mining, or industrial development of any kind is allowed."

At the mention of protected lands, several of the logging company employees shook their head in disapproval.

"In addition, the province has wisely set aside another thirty-two million acres for special management, which means that wildlife habitats, or scenic vistas take precedence over logging."

Willie raised his right arm and gestured to the forest behind him. "The area which these men wish to harvest is unremarkable in that its fish and wildlife are as plentiful and diverse as in many other parts of this great land. And while it is beautiful, it is no more or no less beautiful than any other land the Earth Mother has blessed with her gifts."

Willie paused for a dramatic moment, and in the silence several of the protesters were looking at each other with confused expressions on their faces. He seemed to be making a strong case for the loggers.

"What's going on?" one of them said.

"What's he getting at?" asked another.

"I thought he was on our side."

Like a true professional, Willie's timing was perfect, picking up his speech just as the crowd began to grow noisy.

"But the government of this province is wise and realizes that not all lands requiring protection are extraordinary in terms of their beauty or their wildlife habitats. Some lands must be protected because of their cultural value and importance to the people who call that land their home. These lands . . ." He slowly spread his arms, ". . . are home to the spirits of long-dead hunters and warriors. They hunt alongside the spirits of the bear and the wolf, all the spirits of the animals who have lived and died in these woods through the ages."

A few of the loggers snickered. Noble had to admit that Willie was laying it on a little thick, but it still sounded pretty convincing. Besides, the loggers weren't the ones Willie needed to convince. He needed to get the word out to people all over the province and across the country, especially those in the big cities and centers of government. Who knew what Willie would sound like to them?

"If these lands are violated . . . if the spirits' existence on these lands is disturbed in any way, they will become angry and the peace and harmony of this place will be turned upside down."

Willie nodded, as if he were finished.

One of the loggers stepped forward and shouted. "Is that a threat? Are you threatening us?"

Willie shook his head. "I make no threats. I am only a messenger and my message is this: This land is sacred to my people. It is the home of the spirits of my ancestors. Anger them, and suffer the consequences."

Another logger approached the podium. "So what you're saying is that this land is some sort of ancient Indian burial ground?"

Willie nodded.

The logger and every one of his co-workers laughed. "Oh, that's original. You might as well have told us Freddy Krueger and Jason Voorhees live in those woods."

"Or the Blair Witch," someone called out from the back.

Everyone had a laugh at that, even some of the protesters.

Argus leaned in close to Noble. "This isn't turning out exactly the way we planned."

Noble shook his head. "No, but it's given us something we can work with."

"Like what?" asked Argus.

Noble smiled, but said nothing more.

Chapter 9

"It's time," Noble said, gently shaking Argus awake.

The big teenager groaned and opened his eyes. Noble moved on to Harlan, giving his smaller brother a nudge – and when that didn't work – a playful slap on the cheek.

"Huh? What?" Harlan asked.

"We're going for a run."

"Now?"

"We've got to help Willie."

At the sound of Noble's words, both Argus and Harlan suddenly sat upright, awake and alert. "Is he in trouble?" Argus asked.

"No," answered Noble. "He's all right. But we need to help him with his story."

Harlan rubbed his eyes. "His *story*?"

74

"I'll explain when we get there."

Just then there was a faint knock on the door. The handle turned and the door opened a crack. Tora stood there in her pajamas. "What's going on?"

"We're going for a run," said Noble.

"Now?"

"It's to help Willie," offered Harlan.

Tora nodded, understanding immediately. "I'll meet you out back."

They changed their forms without difficulty. Noble, always the leader, went first, transforming himself into his wolfen form for the long run through the forest. Tora followed, changing from an attractive young woman with a blonde streak in her hair, to a beautiful young wolf with a line of yellow-white fur running down the length of her back. Next came Argus, whose size required that his transformation take twice as long as the others, followed by Harlan, who never missed a chance to show off his newfound shape-shifting abilities. Harlan dove through the air in his human form, landed hands first on the ground, then somersaulted over the earth, rising up on all fours as a compact, slightly bony wolf.

They arrived at the protest site a short time later, possibly around midnight, judging by the position of the nearly full moon. They stopped together behind a line of redwood cedars halfway up a mountainside that allowed them a good view of the site. There was a single light on inside one of the trailers, and by that dim light, and the light of the moon, the pack was able to make out details in the darkness. A lone logger stood guard by the road with a shotgun resting across his folded arms. Obviously Willie's warning that "bad things might happen" had put the company on the alert for some sort of vandalism against Conservco.

That suited the pack just fine.

Noble studied the scene for a while longer, then changed his shape just enough to make himself understood. "Harlan," he said, in a low, gravelly voice. "You need to distract the guard."

Harlan let out a soft growl of understanding.

"Lead him away from the site," Noble continued. "Take him into the woods. Scare him a bit if you have to, just give us a few minutes alone at the site."

Harlan raised and lowered his head and was off, bounding through the woods toward the guard.

Noble turned to Argus and Tora, and said, "This is what we're going to do . . ."

By the time Harlan reached the road, the guard was sitting on a stump with the shotgun across his lap and his head cradled in his hands. He was small for a logger, his work boots and plaid jacket both looking two sizes too big for him. He had a long mullet that curled its way down past his shoulders. Obviously the man had been on duty most of the night, because his eyes were closed and – Harlan listened closely – he seemed to be sound asleep, snoring. If that was the case, it might have been possible for the pack to run quietly through the camp and do whatever it was

76

Noble had in mind, but Harlan knew that if Noble had a plan, it would be a good one, especially if he needed the guard to be out of the picture.

Harlan made his way onto the campsite and hid behind one of the trucks while he figured out the best way to get the man's attention. If he was too loud he'd wake the others, but too quiet and he might not draw the man away from his post. Harlan considered the problem for a few moments, then changed into his human form so he could speak without difficulty.

"Hey Buddy!" he whispered.

The guard did not stir.

"Buddy!" he repeated, this time much louder.

"Huh? Hey!" The man snorted as he awoke. The shotgun shifted in his arms and he juggled it a moment before regaining his grip. "Who's there?"

"It's me," Harlan said, trying to sound as much like a fellow logger as he could. "I couldn't sleep. But I've got a bottle of Canadian Club that'll fix that. Want some?"

The guard gave an exaggerated nod. "A sip of whiskey would go down real nice right about now," he said under his breath. "Maybe even two sips."

Harlan changed back into a wolf and darted away from the site and into the woods. The guard was slow to rise to his feet, and wasted even more time stretching his legs, but eventually he began walking in Harlan's direction. "Where you goin'?" he said.

Harlan stopped in his tracks. The question was a fair one and required an answer . . . and soon. He quickly changed his shape to allow himself speech, then whispered hoarsely, "I don't want the boss man to see us."

"Good thinking," the guard said cheerfully. Harlan could almost hear the man's smile.

Harlan lead the guard into the woods east of the site, but it wasn't long before the man became suspicious.

"Hey, where are you?" he asked. "I can't go too far from camp. I'm still on duty."

Harlan closed the distance between them and growled, low and menacingly, as if he were ready to tear the man's body apart.

"That's not funny," he said, a slash of fear in his voice.

Harlan growled again.

The guard leveled his shotgun at waist height and began to twist his body left and right. "I'll shoot if I have to," he said. "I swear I will."

Harlan had no doubt the man would pull the trigger. Whether or not he'd hit anything was another matter entirely. But even if he did manage to catch Harlan with a blast, as long as the buckshot in the gun wasn't made of silver – which was highly unlikely, since all commercially produced shot is made of lead – the gun could hurt Harlan, but not kill him. Still, gunshots were painful and best avoided if possible. He moved around so that he was between the logger and the campsite, and snarled.

The man ran deeper into the woods, doing his best to weave between the trees and over fallen logs. It was only a matter of time before he stumbled or ran into something he didn't see.

About fifteen seconds to be precise.

A branch jutted out from a spruce at neck height. The logger slammed into it at full speed, his head snapped back, his feet flew out in front of him, and he landed flat on his back. The back of his head absorbed most of the impact. He was out cold.

Harlan smiled as best as his wolfen form would allow. He hadn't planned on this turn of events, but it would certainly do.

While Harlan distracted the guard, Noble, Argus, and Tora closed in on the camp and waited in front of what had become the entrance until Harlan had led the guard into the forest. Once they felt certain the guard would be gone for some time, they moved into the camp.

Noble had explained to them what he had in mind, but he still wasn't sure they'd be able to carry out his plan. It all depended on the size and weight of the equipment scattered around the camp. If it was too heavy he'd have to come up with Plan B. But if there were a few pickup trucks or – even better – cars, his original plan would be fine.

In the center of the camp was an office trailer that Noble figured had a phone, computer, coffee machine, and maybe a few cots for loggers to sleep on. There were two smaller trailers, one of them a faded turquoise, the other the color of a rusty nail. Parked around the perimeter of the camp in a lazy semicircle were some of the company's heavy equipment, including a stripper, a loader, and a Peterbilt tractor with an empty flatbed. They were too

heavy for Noble's use, but fortunately a half-dozen personal vehicles belonging to the loggers were parked around
the three trailers. Four of the vehicles were full-sized
pickup trucks and two of them were fully loaded with
equipment. The third had a diesel fuel tank in its bed, and
the fourth was empty. Of the two remaining vehicles, one
was a small-sized pickup while the other was a four-door
compact car.

That was the one they'd start with.

Noble ran around to the car's front end and changed his
shape. One moment there was a large wolf standing in
front of the car, hind legs on the ground and front legs
resting on the hood. The next moment there was a six-foot
tall werewolf hunched over the front of the car, its body a
mass of rippling muscle and ragged fur. Without a word,
Tora and Argus followed his lead. By far the most impressive change belonged to Argus. Well over six feet in human
form, Argus topped seven feet as a werewolf, his human
form and power seeming to double as he changed shape.
Tora's transformation wasn't as dramatic, but she grew in
size and strength while retaining the distinctive whitish-
yellow streak that flowed down the fur along the back of
her head to just past her shoulders.

"What?" asked Argus, the word coming through as a
rough whisper, as if two pieces of sandpaper had been
rubbed together deep down in his chest to make the word.

Answering the question with words required too much
effort, so Noble used hand gestures to get his message

across. First he pointed to Tora and motioned for her to come around and join him at the front of the car. When she was in place next to him, he raised his hands, palm-up, and signaled that he wanted to flip the car over onto its roof.

Argus looked puzzled, but Noble reassured him with a hand gesture. Argus nodded in response, and moments later the three of them were in position, Noble and Tora at the front of the car, Argus at the rear.

When each of them had a firm grip, Noble nodded his head three times. On the third nod they all lifted in unison.

The wheels on the driver's side of the car came off the ground, but it was obvious that they weren't going to be able to simply turn the car over onto its roof. The car would have to be rolled, which disappointed Noble, since he'd wanted to do this without damaging any of the vehicles . . . or making too much noise.

Oh well, maybe they could get away with just a few dents and scratches, and if somebody heard them, maybe they could all escape before they were seen.

They put the car down and Noble motioned for Argus to take the driver's side while Tora moved around to the rear. Again, Noble counted to three, and on the third count they all lifted together. This time the car rose easily up off the ground, went over onto its side and without much more encouragement, rolled up onto its roof with barely a single dent.

Argus was pleased, the sides of his long, angled snout pulled back to expose a smile full of sharp teeth and fangs.

Noble couldn't help smiling, too. The car had gone over so easily, and with barely a sound, he was eager to try again with one of the heavier vehicles.

They decided on a red pickup truck that had the green Conservco logo on its doors. They needed a symbol that would send a message to the company and this truck would do nicely.

As they'd done before, the three werewolves got into position around the truck, Argus on the driver's side, Tora in back behind the truck's bed, and Noble up front. On the count of three they all lifted, and just like the car had done, the truck went over onto its side and continued rolling until it came to a rest on its roof and hood.

Unlike the car, its weight was distributed unevenly, and as the truck rocked gently back and forth, strange sounds emanated from it as the beams supporting the roof twisted under the tremendous stress.

Something had to give.

The truck's front windshield was the first thing to go. One second the windshield was clear as day, the next it had a crack across it that resembled a lightning bolt. One more second passed and the entire window shattered with a small explosion, frosting over as the glass burst into a thousand tiny shards.

That's when the light came on inside the office trailer.

"What the hell's goin' on out there?" somebody shouted from inside.

Lights in the other trailers came on and doors popped open.

Noble let out an urgent yelp and the three werewolves immediately bolted for the cover of the forest. Noble did his best to change his form as he ran, hoping he could complete the transformation to wolf before any of the loggers could shine a light on them. He was halfway through the change when he saw a beam of light flashing across the trees to his left. With a final leap, he was into the woods, landing on all four of his wolfen legs.

The light continued to sweep the forest, catching trees and bushes behind them and casting scraggly shadows across their bodies. Had they made it into the woods in time? They wouldn't know that till tomorrow, but Noble had an idea that even if the loggers had caught a glimpse of them changing form, it could still work to their advantage.

They circled around the camp and found Harlan watching over the still-unconscious guard.

Noble changed his form so he could speak. "You didn't hurt him, did you?"

Harlan shifted his shape just enough to answer the question. "Funniest thing I've ever seen," he said. "I just growled at him and he ran into a tree."

"We better go," Noble said, turning to leave. "They'll be looking for him."

But before Noble could take a step, Argus put a hand on Noble's shoulder. "Why the cars?" he asked hoarsely, still in his werewolf form.

Noble turned to face his brother. "Remember what Willie said?"

Argus shook his head.

"He said if the company didn't move out, the spirits would become angry and their world would be turned upside down." He paused and cracked a sly smile.

Argus laughed out loud.

The loggers must have heard Argus' laughter because one of them shouted in their direction, "Over there!"

"We better get out of here!" Noble said, bounding into the woods.

The other three followed.

Behind them, a distant voice said, "Buddy, are you okay?"

Chapter 10

The run home was loose and playful, with each member of the pack taking turns leading the way and the rest picking their spots to nudge one another into trees or nip the hind legs of those in front.

Their little adventure had been a complete success. They'd been able to overturn two company vehicles, something that Willie – and hopefully the media – would be able to turn into a really big deal. More importantly, no one had gotten hurt; not a member of the pack, and none of the loggers. If someone were injured, even slightly, the whole nature of the standoff would change from a polite protest to armed conflict. There was a chance someone had seen them as they were making their escape, but even that could work in their favor thanks to Willie's ramblings about awakened spirits in the woods. The protest wasn't over yet, not by a longshot, but the pack had helped the protesters' cause immensely. They hoped it would be enough.

As the pack ran through the woods, Argus fell behind. They were heading home and that meant he'd soon be out of the forest and back in the human world. It was a difficult transition for him to make these days, especially after such an exciting night. Argus's body was still charged with adrenaline, which coursed through him like electricity. How could he possibly change into his human form, slide into bed and sleep the rest of the night?

He wanted to feel Mother Earth beneath his feet. He *needed* to run and hunt . . . to feel blood on his talons and taste its bitter sweetness on his tongue.

Just then, out of the corner of his eye, Argus saw movement in the forest. It was a familiar shape, yet ghostly and eerie in the light and shadows the moon cast upon the forest. He glanced ahead to see if the others had noticed, but he'd been lagging behind for so long that they were no longer in sight. He was alone now and the vision he'd seen before was nearby, so close he could actually feel its presence.

Argus left the path, leaping through the trees to the right and charging through the forest in the direction of the apparition.

The pack was nearly home when they realized Argus wasn't with them. They stopped and waited on the path, thinking their bigger brother would be along at any moment, but after several minutes it was obvious that they'd lost him . . . or he'd gone off on his own somewhere. Either way, Noble was concerned. It wasn't like Argus to just go without telling them, especially since the last time one of them had ventured off alone Tora had ended up locked in a cage by a mad scientist determined to steal her from the forest. After that, they had vowed to stick together and it was unlike Argus, of all people, to be the first to break that promise.

Noble nudged Harlan and gestured along the trail in the direction they'd just come. Harlan was the best tracker of the pack and if Argus had left the path, Harlan would be able to find him – hopefully before something bad happened.

Harlan nodded, turned around and set his snout low to the ground. Noble and Tora waited for him to find their scent. After a moment he was off, sniffing the trail in search of his bigger brother, with Noble and Tora close behind.

Argus wasn't sure where he was in the forest. He knew he was in the area being disputed by the logging company and the protesters, but other than that he was lost. He'd been so intent on finding the apparition that he hadn't paid attention to where he was or where he was going. Now it all seemed foreign to him, as if he'd been dropped into a strange land where he did not belong.

Suddenly, there to the left . . . movement between the trees. Argus caught a glimpse of something large making its way through the forest, but when he turned to take a better look the thing was gone. Only the swaying of branches told him that something had been there a moment before.

He ran over to the trees, still now, but holding the key to finding the apparition. There was a strange, yet somehow familiar scent on the leaves.

Argus didn't understand. The scent was strong enough that even he could track it, but what it was telling him didn't make any sense.

Or did it?

Still in his wolfen form, he followed the trail as best he could, keeping his snout low to the ground, appreciating Harlan's tracking ability more and more with each step. The scent was getting stronger now, and becoming even more of a mystery.

The trail abruptly ended at a fair-sized redwood. Argus sniffed the base of the tree until he realized that the scent hadn't ended there, but had merely changed direction.

Up!

Argus lifted his head to look along the trunk of the tree – just in time to see a large werewolf plunging through the branches, its maw open, teeth bared, and its scraggly hair trailing behind it like the frayed threads of a flag.

There was no time to move. Barely time to brace for the impact.

Thhhump!

Argus was pinned to the ground by two massive arms connected to a body that was much bigger and heavier than his own. The werewolf's fangs were bared in a snarl and Argus was amazed at the length and sharpness of them. Any one of those teeth could tear through his neck in a single bite.

"Who are you?" the werewolf rasped.

Argus *tried* to answer, but the beast was sitting too heavily on his chest. He couldn't get enough air to breathe, let alone answer a question.

"What do you want?"

Again, Argus did his best to make a sound, but it was impossible.

Sensing the problem, the massive werewolf eased up on Argus, allowing him a much-needed gulp of air . . . but only one.

"Well?" he asked again, lowering his weight back down upon Argus's chest.

Not knowing what else to do, Argus changed the form of his upper body just enough to enable him to speak. "Ar-guss!" he wheezed. "Ar-r-guss Brock."

The werewolf sneered under his breath. "You're a long way from home, Argus Brock!"

Harlan had followed Argus's scent deep into the forest. As it grew stronger and more fresh, he became certain they'd find Argus at any moment.

But then Harlan stopped in his tracks. Up ahead he heard voices. Harsh, rough voices. Voices that weren't human.

Noble had heard them too. They were too deep into the woods to come across any human, even a logger. It was a bizarre thought, but voices this far-removed from Redstone could only mean . . .

Noble crept forward, hoping to catch a glimpse of whoever was speaking.

There, in a clearing, lay Argus in his werewolf form. He was pinned down by another werewolf, bigger than Argus by half. There was a look of fear on his brother's face, an expression the pack had so rarely seen on him that it appeared unnatural.

There was no time to lose, thought Noble. Yes, this other creature was one of their kind, but there was no telling what it might do to Argus. It would be a difficult task for them to overpower this larger beast and free their brother, but once they pounced, Argus would likely join the fight. Four against one seemed like pretty good odds.

Noble transformed into his werewolf form and gestured to the others to do the same.

Within seconds Noble, Tora, and Harlan were ready for the attack. Without a word, Noble directed Harlan to the far side of the clearing, and Tora to the right, directly behind the massive werewolf. On Noble's command, they would all strike at once. After that, who knew . . . .

Noble counted to three, then sprang forward, flying through the air toward the big werewolf, talons and fangs bared. A split second later, Harlan came bounding through the bushes with a roar. Then Tora leaped on the beast's back, claws ready to rake the creature's face and slice it wide open.

"Wait! No!" Argus cried.

Noble relaxed immediately, but did not release his hold on the beast's neck.

"Stop!" said Argus. "This is Phelan. He was a member of our parents' pack. He knew our mother and father."

Noble's arms and legs weakened. He lost his grip on the beast and hit the ground with a loud, hard *thud*.

Chapter 11

"Your father's name was Ohdin, your mother's was Mahra," said Phelan. He was a man . . . a werewolf of few words. He had the ability to speak well enough, but the formation of words seemed difficult, as if he hadn't used that ability for a long time. He answered the pack's questions as best he could, but he never offered any more than was asked of him. As a result, the pack had to draw information from him bit by bit.

"Where did they live?" asked Tora.

"Here," Phelan said, gesturing the forest to his right. "There," he said, gesturing to his left. Then he spread both arms wide. "Everywhere."

"Were they good fighters?" Argus wanted to know.

A smile stretched over Phelan's face. "Your father was alpha male. The most ferocious fighter in all the packs north of this place." There was obvious pride in Phelan's gruff voice, and perhaps a bit of sorrow in their passing.

Argus smiled as well. It made him feel good to know that he'd taken after his father in this very important way.

"Were they smart?" asked Harlan.

"Yes," Phelan nodded. "Once, a ranger left behind his light here in the woods. Your father knew what it was, and how to make the light appear. He used it well until it died."

Harlan looked confused. Here was Phelan telling them how smart their father was because he knew how to work a flashlight, something that didn't take a genius to figure out. Harlan didn't get it, but Noble understood just fine. Phelan was a werewolf, a beast, a creature of the wild. He was more wolf than man and he would always be that way. Having been raised by Ranger Brock and Phyllis had changed the pack, made them more human than wolf. Noble hated to use the word because it sounded as if it was a slight against Phelan and his kind, but the pack had become more *civilized* by living amongst humans. Phelan was like an ancestor to them, as if there were generations and generations between them rather than just one.

"What about our mother?" Tora asked.

"You remind me of her." Phelan nodded. "She was sleek. Elegant. And she had the same stripe in her hair as you."

Noble looked to the ground, beginning to feel uneasy about what Phelan was saying. It all seemed too good to be true. Their father was the smartest, fastest, toughest wolf in all the British Columbia forests, and their mother was the most beautiful, refined, blah, blah, blah . . .

Everything was so wonderful, and Noble knew that that simply wasn't the case. If their parents had been so great, where were they now? Why did the pack have to be raised by Phyllis and Ranger Brock? And why did so much responsibility for the pack have to fall on *his* shoulders? He was a teenager just like the others, but somehow he never felt like one.

"What happened to them?" he said. "If our parents were as smart and strong as you say, then how did they get caught in the fire? Why did they have to die?"

Harlan, Tora, and Argus all looked at Noble with a variety of shocked, angry glances. To his credit, Phelan wasn't bothered by Noble's question in the least. In fact, he seemed pleased to answer it.

"You must be alpha male, eh? You are wary. Unbelieving." He nodded his head. "That is a good way to think, but not forever. A time comes when you must believe so the anger and hurt in here –" He touched a talon-tipped finger to his heart, "– can go away."

Noble suddenly felt ashamed. For as much as he enjoyed being the pack's leader, there were times when he wished for nothing more than to be a follower. He rarely got that chance, and deep down inside he felt a bit of resentment toward his parents for placing him in that position. No matter how heroic they'd been in death, they'd still left the survival of the pack to fate and the kindness of a single man. Somehow, Phelan understood all that, and had been able to draw it out of Noble with just a few simple words.

"You know of the fire," Phelan said. It was both a statement and a question.

"The ranger told us the story of how he found us and brought us home," said Tora.

"Ah, the ranger," said Phelan. "He is a good man. He works to save this . . ." He gestured to the forest around him. "That is a rare thing in their kind."

"But how did the ranger come to find us?" Harlan asked. "What happened before that?"

Phelan was silent a moment, while he composed his thoughts. Then, after a deep breath, he began. "Your mother was already in the process of birthing you when we smelled the smoke." A ripple of sorrow coursed through his body. "We thought there would be time for her to birth all the cubs before the fire came, but . . ." He shook his head slowly. "The fire was angry and ravenous. There was no time for anything but to run . . . run for our lives." He paused again to take several breaths and steady himself. "Your father told us to go. He told us he would stay with your mother until all of you were born."

Noble stared at Phelan, desperate to ask the question. But before he could gather the courage, Argus asked for each of them.

"Were there only four?"

Phelan shook his head. "No."

Tora gasped. Harlan sniffed. Argus crossed his arms and closed his eyes for a long moment.

Noble knew what they were thinking. His heart felt as if it had been torn open by the thought of there being more of them. A brother? A sister? Dead. They had been the lucky ones. Born first and alive because of it. A twinge of guilt crept up Noble's spine. Perhaps he was not the pack's natural leader. Maybe there had been another brother born after him who would have been smarter and stronger, only to perish before he took his first breath.

And suddenly, Noble felt a deep and profound regret. How could he have questioned his parents' actions so readily? How could he have been so selfish as to resent being thrust into the role of leader, thinking it had been foisted upon him by his parents when, in reality, it had been a cruel turn of fate.

"Your father carried away the cubs as they were born. He was able to save the four of you. He died in the fire, along with your mother, trying to save the fifth."

Everyone was silent for the longest time.

Finally it was Tora who broke the silence with another question. "How could you know this? How could you live and know what happened to them at the end?"

Phelan nodded. "It is a fair question. Sometimes I wonder why I lived and they had to die, but it was your father's doing. I stayed with Mahra while she birthed you, but by the time the fifth cub was coming the flames were too hot and too close to remain. Ohdin told me to go . . . *ordered* me to go, saying he would stay with your mother until the last of the cubs was born." A slight shake of his head. "Ohdin could have lived too, if he'd run at that

moment, but he stayed by Mahra's side. I think he preferred to die with her than live without her."

"If you knew all this, why didn't you find us before
now?" Tora sounded angry, and to be honest, amidst his
own mix of emotions, Noble felt a bit of that anger, too.

"Your father knew what he was doing when he carried
you out of the fire. I don't know if he *chose* your Ranger
Brock, but it wouldn't surprise me if he had. He always
did things for a reason. The ranger has been good for you.
He's raised you well."

Tora was staring off into the distance. "We always
thought we were freaks . . . the only ones." She looked
Phelan in the eye. "Why didn't you show yourself to us
before this?"

"You were not ready to know the truth."

"And now we are?" Argus said.

Phelan nodded. "I think so."

Harlan leaned forward on the log he was sitting on.
"Tell us more about our parents," he said. "I want to know
everything."

Phelan took a deep breath, and told them a story. There
were dozens of them, stories that stretched long into the
night.

Eventually, rays of sunshine appeared through the trees
and it was time for the pack to return home.

"Come back any time," Phelan said, as they parted.

"I will," said Argus, then corrected himself. "We will."

Chapter 12

The pack made it to school on time the next morning with the assistance of Phyllis. She asked each of them where they'd been all night, but no one was saying and Phyllis knew enough not to ask twice. More questions would have gotten her nowhere since Noble had instructed the pack not to mention anything about Phelan just yet. If the others felt the same way Noble did, then their meeting with Phelan had unleashed a complicated set of emotions within each of them. In Phelan they had found one of their own who knew their parents and could tell them and show them things Ranger Brock could never even imagine. But Ranger Brock and Phyllis had taken them in and raised them, had shown them love and compassion when they were at their most vulnerable. If Phelan knew they'd been taken in by Ranger Brock, then why hadn't he come for them, retrieved them and taken them back to the forest to be among their kind?

So many questions . . . .

Noble hoped they would all be answered in time, either by Ranger Brock or Phelan. Between the two of them lay all the facts and when the time was right the pack would have the answers they were looking for. But not now. Right now they had other things to deal with . . . like high school.

"We're here!" said Phyllis in something close to a shout.

Mumblings and grumblings from throughout the car as the four members of the pack woke up.

"Already?" asked Harlan.

"You sure this is our school?" Argus chimed in.

Tora and Noble said nothing, taking the opportunity instead to rub the sleep from their eyes. The drive to school took only twenty minutes, but Noble felt like he'd been asleep for hours.

"Don't skip any classes," Phyllis said as they piled out of the car.

"We won't," answered Noble, already wondering which ones he could afford to miss in favor of sleep in the boys locker room.

"I'm sure," Phyllis said skeptically. When the car doors were all closed she waved and drove off.

The pack turned and began the long walk up the school steps. There was still ten minutes before classes started and they would need every one of them to get to where they were going.

They'd nearly reached the front doors when Jake
MacKinnon and six of his toadies suddenly appeared from
behind a stand of cedar bushes.

"Well, if it isn't Dogface and the rest of the litter."

Dogface!

Noble felt the hair standing up on the back of his neck.
He saw that MacKinnon's words were having a similar
effect on Tora and Argus. In fact, Argus had balled his
hands into fists to hide his growing talons and the hair
sprouting on his knuckles. He could hardly imagine what
Harlan was feeling right now.

"Not today, MacKinnon," Harlan said. "I'm not in the
mood."

MacKinnon and his friends laughed. "Not in the
mood?" Jake said, his face all twisted as if he didn't understand Harlan's response. "I don't want to kiss you . . . I
just want to talk."

More laughter and catcalls.

"Who'd want to kiss that?" someone said.

"And you don't know where that mouth has been," said
another. "Probably, drinking out of the toilet."

The laughter continued as more and more students
gathered around.

Noble looked over at his brother. It was obvious from
the way Harlan was filling out his clothing that he was
allowing parts of his body to transform, making himself
stronger in case there was a fight. While there was no
doubt that Harlan could take MacKinnon in such a form,

Lone Wolf

it was extremely dangerous to the rest of the pack. He could control his transformations under ideal conditions, but in a fight there was no way to be sure Harlan wouldn't fully change himself into a werewolf. And if that happened, the pack's life as they knew it would be over. Even escape into the forests wouldn't be safe.

Harlan let the laughter die down, then said, "All you ever want to do is talk, MacKinnon." He shook his head. "You know, I've never heard someone talk so much, yet say so little."

A murmur coursed through the crowd.

MacKinnon took a step forward. "I usually let my fists do the talking, asshole! But you're too yellow to fight. Ha! Maybe that's what I should call you. *Old Yeller*!"

Another dog reference.

The laughter this time was more subdued. Snickers and giggles instead of wide-open guffaws.

Harlan looked as if his inner wolf was about to break through his shirt and tear Jake into wet little pieces. Argus too, was ready to pounce, half-crouched with his clawed hands curled, ready to separate MacKinnon's head from his shoulders.

"I bet you like to suck eggs too!"

That was it, the final straw.

Harlan dropped his books and stepped forward, ready for a fight.

"Well, all right," MacKinnon said, dropping his knapsack and taking a step toward Harlan.

The rest of the students automatically closed in around them, forming a ring that would set the boundaries of the fight.

Noble would have liked to see Harlan beat the crap out of Jake. After all, if anyone deserved a beating, it was him. But there was no way Harlan could take him without at least partially transforming into his werewolf form, and Noble couldn't let Harlan do that to the rest of the pack.

Noble turned to Argus and flicked his head in Harlan's direction. "Stop them!"

Without a moment's hesitation, Argus was in the center of the ring of students, standing between Harlan and Jake, blocking their access to each other.

"Get out of here, Argus!" Harlan said. "Let me do this!"

Argus said nothing, and did not move.

"Oh, this is rich," Jake whined. "You need your big brother to fight your battles for you?"

"Argus, I mean it," Harlan said, trying to get his brother out of the way, but having as much success as if he were moving a redwood.

"Yeah, c'mon, brother bear," Jake said. "I promise not to hurt your little brother . . . much."

Argus slowly turned, his fists clenching and unclenching. "You looking to fight me, too?" he asked.

"Hey," he said. Jake raised his arms into the air. "This is between me and Dogface. He wants a fight as badly as I do!"

Argus looked over at Noble for guidance.

There was no way out of this, Noble knew. If they didn't settle this, it could go on for months . . . until they graduated high school. Even then it might never end.

"You want to fight Harlan?" Noble said.

"Yeah," Jake answered. "I do."

"Fine –"

The crowd of students gasped.

Harlan looked at Noble with surprise written all over his face.

"All right!" Jake said, pumping a fist into the air.

"You can fight my brother," Noble said, his voice calm, his words measured, "One-on-one with no interference from any of us."

MacKinnon began to roll up his sleeves.

"But not now," Noble added.

"What?"

"Tomorrow. After school."

MacKinnon shook his head in disappointment. "Oh, come on."

Noble jabbed a thumb to his right.

Principal Terashita was coming up the steps to the school. "What's going on here?" he asked.

"Just a friendly chat, sir," Noble said.

The principal's face suddenly broke into a smile. Noble was one of his favorite students and anything he said was always taken at face value.

"Well there'll be plenty of time for talk later. Let's get into the school before we're *all* late for class."

The students began moving.

Jake made his way over to the pack. "Tomorrow, Dogface," he said. "Your ass is mine!"

When MacKinnon was gone, Harlan looked at Noble with narrowed eyes. "You've got a plan, right?"

Noble smiled. "Don't I always?"

"Yeah. I'm just checking."

The bell rang to start the school day.

"C'mon," said Noble. "I'll fill you in on the way to class."

Chapter 13

The pack tried hard to catch up on their sleep during lunch and study periods. It didn't make up for the night of lost sleep, but it was enough to keep them all going for the next little while.

When school ended, Ranger Brock was in his 4×4 waiting for them in the parking lot.

"I heard you had a late night yesterday," he said, as they neared his vehicle.

"Not that late," offered Tora.

"Yeah," said Harlan. "We were in bed by . . . well, before breakfast, anyway."

The ranger nodded as if he were unconcerned. "I'm heading up to the protest site. Willie is going to do another press conference and I thought you might want to hear what he has to say."

"You bet."

"Sure."

"Let's go!"

It was a ten-minute drive on the highway, and then another ten minutes along the narrow dirt road. If the logging company wanted to use this road on a regular basis, they were going to have to widen it.

Long before they reached the site, they noticed additional cars parked along the right side of the road.

"Where did all these cars come from?" asked Argus.

Harlan cracked a smile. "I hear there's a factory that makes them in Oshawa . . . . That's in Ontario."

Argus made a fist and punched his smaller brother in the arm.

"Ow."

The closer they got to the site, the more cars there were.

"I expected more people here today," said Ranger Brock, "but I had no idea there'd be this many."

"Maybe something happened in the night," said Noble, sitting in the front passenger seat of the 4×4. As he spoke, he turned to look at the others in the backseat, then gave them a smile and a quick thumbs up.

"Gee," said Harlan, still rubbing his arm. "I wonder what it could have been."

"Look!" cried Tora.

They were still nearing the site, but even at this distance the two overturned cars could clearly be seen, looking for all the world like two fish out of water.

Ranger Brock found a spot to park and all five of them got out of the vehicle. Willie was standing at the podium just like he'd done the day before, but this time there were all kinds of microphones and tape recorders in front of him. Other reporters stood close by with pens and notebooks in hand, frantically scribbling Willie's words down as if they were prophecies about the end of the world.

"Last night," he said, in an even more compelling voice he'd obviously rehearsed, "the spirits spoke to me. They told me they were unhappy. Their world . . ." A pause for effect, ". . . has been violated. Turned upside down. So, they have begun to fight back . . ." He spread his arms, gesturing at the two overturned vehicles, ". . . turning the world of these men upside down." He crossed his arms over his chest, in an attempt to make himself look powerful and steadfast. Noble winced at the move, thinking it made him look more like a wooden cigar store Indian than anything else. "It is a warning. If they stay here on these lands any longer, there could be worse things to come."

Argus looked at Noble as if asking for an explanation.

Noble shrugged. All they had done was give Willie a little something to back up his claims, and now he was running with it. As long as he kept his predictions vague and non-violent, the pack would be able to back him up with some sort of mysterious occurrences.

The moment Willie finished speaking, a dozen hands went up and every reporter there was shouting his name.

"Manchoka!"

Edo van Belkom

Willie pointed to the reporter and camera crew from the CBC, then glanced over at Noble and winked.

Noble laughed under his breath. It appeared that Willie had finally landed the role of a lifetime and was giving an award-calibre performance.

"Could you be a little more specific about the nature of these spirits?" asked the pretty young reporter. "What are their names? Their backgrounds? And how could they possibly overturn such heavy vehicles?"

"Uh oh," muttered Argus.

"Well, that's that," stated Tora.

Harlan looked at his two siblings. "Hey, I'd like to know that myself."

Noble refrained from saying anything. He was confident in Willie's ability as an actor. Surely he'd done some homework and devised a backup story for his "spirits." And then, right on cue, Willie launched into a story about an ancient chief.

"His name was Nonokoot," he said, as if he were retelling a legend around the campfire after a hunt. "And his daughter was the most beautiful creature on these lands . . ."

Noble listened, and smiled. Willie was so convincing, Noble almost believed the story himself.

And the cameras kept rolling. The tape players kept recording.

"Will you listen to that guy!" fumed Tyler Allen Ceballo from inside the Conservco company trailer. He turned

108

away from the window where he'd been watching Willie Greene give his press conference and shook his head in disgust. "I've never heard such a load of crap in all my life. Angry spirits, my foot! The only spirits he's seen lately are the ones that come out of a bottle."

A few of the men inside the trailer laughed. The rest looked at him with uncomfortable expressions on their faces.

"All he's doing is playing us like a cheap guitar!" Ceballo said, beginning to pace the room. "If these woods are haunted, then my name is Sitting Bull!"

"Well, you can say what you want," said Grant Willem, the company's number two man on the site. "But Bobby did see something weird last night."

"What? What did he see?" Ceballo shouted. "I've asked the man a dozen times to tell me what he saw, and all he can say is gibberish about big hairy creatures." He let out a sigh. "For all I know he was into the spirits last night too."

"You can badmouth him all you want," Willem said, his tone even and calm. "But *something* was on-site last night and turned over a couple of our cars."

Ceballo bent at the waist until he was eye to eye with the seated Willem. "*Something!* Some-*thing* didn't do anything last night; it was those protesters. They snuck up here, scared the pants off our so-called security guard, and then they rolled our cars. That's all that happened . . . Nothing more!" He finished off his words by looking around the room, making eye contact with everyone in the trailer.

Grant Willem was unshaken by Ceballo's intimidation. "Yeah, well even if that's *all* it was, that's still pretty impressive. How many people do you think it would take to turn over one of those vehicles? Ten? Fifteen?" He shrugged. "However many it took, they managed to get up here, turn over the cars, and get away again without waking any of us up. I'd say that's something to be worried about."

Several of the other loggers nodded in agreement.

Ceballo crossed his arms over his chest, smiled in an angry sort of way – with the corners of his mouth forming a hint of a grimace – then began pacing the room and shaking his head. "I don't believe this! I don't believe what I'm hearing. You guys are supposed to be lumberjacks . . . big, tough, smelly lumberjacks for crying out loud! And here you are afraid of the conjurings of some crackpot and a platoon of blue-haired, tree-hugging old ladies." He uncrossed his arms and put his hands on the shoulders of two men sitting in front of him. "C'mon now . . . we've been through stuff like this before. Remember Port Simpson and Alice Arm? Things started off rough there too, but we stuck it out. These people are salad-eaters who are up here protesting, not because they love the environment, but because they feel guilty about destroying it. They'll be here a few more days shoutin' their slogans and wavin' their flags, but they'll get tired of it sooner or later. Then they'll drive back to the city in their gas-guzzling SUVs, satisfied they did what they could. That'll leave just the people who live around here. They might take a bit longer to wear down, but once they realize how much money's at stake, how many jobs are waiting for them . . . they'll come around." The angry edge to his smile was gone now, and he managed a little laugh under his breath. "And if they still want to put up a fight, we can always buy their support with more cash and drinks."

The room was silent for a moment. Finally somebody said, "What about after?"

"What do you mean?"

"What about after we're finished with the forest here? What then?"

Ceballo looked at the man as if he couldn't believe someone could ask such a stupid question. "What's your name?"

"Brian," he said. "Brian McAteer."

"And how long have you been with us?"

"Ten months . . . almost a year."

"Well, Brian. When we're done here, we'll move somewhere else and do it all over again." A pause. "It's what we do."

"Oh." McAteer said the word like he understood, but the look on his face suggested he didn't.

"Now," Ceballo continued. "We just need to stick it out a few more days, a week at the most. By then all these people will be gone. After that, if everything goes well, we can probably start harvesting by the end of the month, maybe the next."

He paused a moment to look around the room. "So who's with me? Who's for showing these bumpkins that

Conservco loggers don't scare easily, that we can give as good as we get, and then some?"

A couple of hands went up.

"There's bonuses in it for everyone who stays on . . . and an extra two hundred bucks for each man who spends a night on watch with a shotgun."

Every hand in the trailer was high in the air.

"Good," Ceballo said. "That's more like it. If the people around here want to play rough, we can play rougher."

The bus was big and yellow, and made a lot of noise as it chugged up the road toward the protest site. There were arms sticking out of the windows on each side, ending in clenched fists or waving little Canadian flags.

The bus skidded to a stop at the edge of the protest site and for a moment was almost totally obscured by a cloud of dust. When the dust settled, the doors opened and people began filing out, one by one.

"Who are they?" Argus asked.

Noble took a closer look at the bus and read the banner draped across its side. "Says they're from some writers' union."

"What's this protest got to do with writing?" Harlan asked.

Noble shrugged. "Who knows?" he said. "Let's just be glad they're here."

Chapter 14

After supper, the pack slid into their beds and slept until well after dark. Noble was the first to awaken, gently arousing the others without disturbing Ranger Brock and Phyllis.

Turning over a couple of cars had been good for the protesters cause, but it had done very little to convince the loggers that they should seriously think about harvesting another section of forest farther away from town. The public opinion war over the site was at a stalemate with an equal number of people for and against the logging company's plans. The deadlock was misleading, since it was common knowledge that Conservco was paying their supporters to be there and was busing people in from out of town whenever the number of protesters grew. That bit of news hadn't been reported on television yet, since there was no hard evidence to prove there was any foul play going on. Besides, none of the journalists working the site seemed interested in that side of the story, choosing instead to focus on Willie Greene and his angry spirits. Sure, it was a bit of a circus, but the circus was keeping the story in the news and as long as that was happening, the support for Donna Hughson and her group would likely grow. Eventually, Conservco would have no choice but to concede the land and move their operation onto the other side of the river.

"Harlan, wake up!" Noble whispered, giving his smaller brother's shoulder a gentle shake.

"What? What is it?"

"We've got to go back up to the site."

"I don't want to go back up there," Harlan moaned. "It doesn't matter what we do, they'll just bring in more people from Prince George."

"We're not going to turn over any cars tonight," Noble said. "We don't need more support."

"No? Then what?"

"We're going to divide and conquer."

Argus was lying on his side, his head cradled in his open hand. "Oh, I like the sound of that."

Noble turned. "You're going to like this a lot."

Harlan crawled out of bed. "I'll get Tora."

They reached the protest site around midnight. There was a good-sized moon hanging over the mountains, but they wouldn't be needing it to find their way around. The loggers had lights up throughout the camp and the constant hum of a generator could be heard in the distance. The lights hadn't turned night into day, but it was more than enough for the guards to see any trespassers entering the camp.

"What now?" asked Tora in the harsh voice of her werewolf form.

The pack had been watching the camp from a safe distance, and if the lights weren't enough to put a stop to their plans, there were at least six men on guard duty, each carrying a shotgun or rifle.

Noble hesitated. "Let me think."

Argus chuckled under his breath. "You mean Noble Brock doesn't have a back-up plan?"

Both Harlan and Tora looked at Argus.

Noble sensed an edge to Argus's voice, as if he were making fun of his smaller brother, or resented his brother's role as leader of the pack. Whatever the problem, it would have to be addressed later. Right now, Noble had to come up with something or the night would be wasted. A few moments later he had it.

"Wait here for my signal," he said, already heading down the slope toward the camp.

"What's the signal?" Tora asked.

But Noble had changed into his wolfen form and was unable to answer. Not to worry, he thought. They'll know it when they see it.

Noble took his time getting down to the campsite. He was a wolf in the woods . . . nothing unusual about that. Nor was there anything unusual about a wolf visiting the site. Wolves were curious creatures, and it stood to reason that all the activity in the area might draw their attention. But how close would a wolf get to satisfy its curiosity? That's where Noble would diverge from the norm and do something unexpected.

He moved as quietly through the woods as he could until he was within earshot of the guard sitting on a wooden box – possibly full of ammunition – in front of the company trailer. There was a light on over the door of the trailer that lit a large circle of ground all around it. When Noble was sure the guard could hear him, he stepped on a good-sized branch with his front paw, snapping it in two.

"Who's there?" the man asked, getting up off his box and peering into the woods.

Noble stepped on a piece of the branch, making another snapping noise – this one louder than the first.

"You've got about two seconds to tell me who's there, or I swear I'll put a load of lead right into your ass!"

Certain he had the man's attention, Noble stepped out from the woods and into the pool of light.

The man's eyes grew wide, but his face registered no fear. Why should it? Noble was just a wolf, and the man did have a gun after all.

"Well, I'll be," he said with a hint of a laugh.

Noble stood still on all fours, trying hard to put the right expression on his face – curiosity and surprise, but only a tiny hint of fear. This was *their* home, after all, and the loggers were the ones who were out of place in the forest.

"You're a good-looking fella, aren't you?"

Noble resisted the urge to smile. He'd been told by many people that he was a handsome boy and the attention of all the girls at school supported that. As a wolf, however, Noble was merely average. His black-gray features seemed plain compared to the streak of white fur that ran down Tora's back, and he was small next to Argus, who was easily the most impressive looking wolf in the pack, especially with one blue eye and one green.

He took a cautious step forward.

"Here boy," the man said, as if he were calling a dog. It would have been cute if he hadn't kept the barrel of his gun pointed at Noble the entire time.

Noble took a tentative step forward.

The gun jerked slightly and the barrel was now pointed at his head. It was a dangerous situation to say the least. No one would condemn the logger for shooting a wolf that ventured into their camp, and while a shotgun blast was survivable if there was no silver in the ammunition, at this range it would likely cause permanent damage to Noble's face and brain.

Noble took a step to the side, as if he were going around the man.

"Bang!" the man said aloud.

Noble cringed and pulled back.

The man started to laugh.

Noble regained his composure and took another step to the side . . . and another, and another. Soon he was around the man and the trailer, heading through the campsite.

Noble heard the man laughing heartily for a while until the sound was drowned out by the generator behind the trailer.

Noble changed his form enough to give him hands and fingers. There was an *on/off* switch on one side of the generator, but that was too simple. If he switched the generator off, it could easily be turned back on in seconds. He needed something more that would give the pack at least an hour of darkness. He looked on the other side of the generator and saw a jumble of wires leading to the lights strung up around the site.

Noble switched the generator *off*. It died after just a few seconds. The lights around the camp slowly began to dim. The man's laughter could be heard for a moment over the dying generator, then, "What the –"

Noble grabbed the wires connected to the generator . . . and pulled.

In an instant, the camp was shrouded in darkness.

"That must be the signal," Harlan said.

Tora shook her head. "I can't believe he walked right into the camp like that. He could have been killed."

Argus nodded. "He's either braver than he let's on, or he's not as smart as we think."

"Never mind that now," said Harlan. "Let's go."

The three of them headed down toward the camp, transforming not into wolves, but into their full werewolf form.

The plan was simple. If there were angry spirits in these woods, then it was time for them to show their anger.

With the lights out, the camp had become a mass of confusion. Some loggers ran, shouting for the generator, while others produced flashlights with beams that cut through the darkness like blades of light.

Argus was the first to pounce. He leaped onto the back of a logger, knocking the man to the ground and sending his shotgun tumbling to the dirt. The man was knocked senseless by the force of the blow, but that didn't stop Argus from turning the guy over and tearing his clothes from his body.

Noble had been very specific in his instructions; they were out to raise a little hell. They could scare the crap out of anyone they wanted, as long as they didn't so much as cause a single scratch on anybody. It was tough to frighten someone without hurting them, but that just made it more of a challenge.

When the man opened his eyes, Argus lowered his face until there were scant inches between them. The man blinked a couple of times, then Argus opened his maw and let out the loudest, most terrifying roar he could.

The man's hair was blown back by the blast and his eyes began to water.

Argus rose up on all fours and the man cowered beneath him, expecting something large and heavy to fall on top of him. Argus wanted to tear the man apart limb by limb, but knew he couldn't. As much as he felt an urge to break bones and rend flesh, Argus kept his instincts in check. Instead of hitting him again, Argus picked up the shotgun and pointed it at the logger.

The man shuddered as a large, wet stain slowly appeared in the crotch of his jeans.

Argus let out a snort, then took the gun barrel in his hands and bent it. The man was sobbing now. Satisfied there was one less logger to worry about, Argus tossed the gun aside and moved on to his next victim.

Tora leaped off the roof of a trailer, hitting the guard square in the left shoulder and knocking him face down on the road. She hovered over him as he lay on his stomach groaning in pain.

She was tempted to leave him there, but while she'd knocked him down and out, there was really nothing for the man to be afraid of. He didn't know what had hit him, and since the whole purpose of this exercise was to instill fear in the loggers, she waited for the man to get up. When he didn't, she grabbed the collar of his jacket and stood him up.

"Thanks," he said, his back still to Tora. "One minute I'm standing there and the next thing I'm on the ground chewing on a mouthful of dirt." He shook his head. "I don't know what the hell hit me."

Tora turned him around, lifted him off the ground and said, "I did."

"Holy sh –"

Tora threw him down. He struggled to get to his feet, and when he was finally upright she gave him a good hard kick in the butt. He flew several feet through the air and hit the ground running . . .

And he kept running until he was far, far away.

Harlan was having some fun of his own.

His guy was facing the road by the edge of the camp, on guard against any blue-haired old ladies who might sneak up on him in the middle of the night to give him a hug.

Harlan crept up behind him without a sound. Then standing just inches away, he began to breathe on the logger's neck.

He could hear the man's breath getting ragged as he was slowly overcome by fear.

"Get out!" Harlan whispered into his ear. "We spirits are angry."

The man was afraid, no doubt about it, but that wasn't enough. He needed to be *very* afraid. So Harlan reached down inside the man's pants and took hold of his underwear. Then with all the strength he could muster, Harlan pulled . . . and pulled.

The man was lifted two feet off the ground as a good eighteen inches of underwear suddenly appeared above his waistline.

"Ah, ow!" the man screamed.

"Get out!" Harlan whispered.

"I'm gone! I'm gone!" the man screamed.

Harlan set him back down. He howled with laughter as the man ran away, his legs bowed while a white underwear flag flapped in the breeze behind him.

If only, thought Harlan, *I could do the same thing to Jake MacKinnon.*

When they were done, the campsite was a shamble. There were men running every which way and several of the protesters who'd been camping out down the road had dropped by to see what all the commotion was about.

"We're done," Noble told Harlan. "Pass it along."

Minutes later the pack was safely back in the forest, high-fiving each other and laughing at the havoc they'd caused.

"That'll convince them that the *spirits* are angry," said Harlan.

"May-be," Argus said, drawing the word out in two full syllables. There was a strange tone to his voice, as if all the fun had made him sad somehow.

"What do you mean maybe?" Tora cried. "You should've seen my guy run."

Argus nodded. "I bet he was scared."

Again, that hadn't sounded right. Usually, after such episodes, Argus would be the one howling with delight. But here he was acting as if a friend had died, or he'd lost all hope.

Noble stepped forward. "You okay, Argus?"

"Huh, what?" Argus snapped, as he suddenly realized he'd been wearing his emotions on his sleeve. "Yeah, I'm fine."

"You sure?"

He shrugged. "I guess scaring people isn't as much fun as it used to be."

"*I'll* never get tired of it," said Harlan.

Noble and Tora laughed. Argus's expression remained unchanged.

"C'mon," said Noble. "We've still got time to get a few hours of sleep in before school."

The pack readied for the run home. All except for Argus who lingered in the forest as if he planned to stay out all night.

"C'mon Argus," cheered Noble. "First one home gets to call in sick for school tomorrow."

"Eat my dust," cried Harlan, transforming to wolfen form and bounding into the forest. Tora followed her brother, but Noble waited for Argus to join in.

"You go on ahead," Argus said. "I want to be alone for a while."

Noble did not move. "It's Phelan, isn't it?"

Argus nodded. "I want to talk to him."

"We all want to do that," said Noble.

"No, it's more than that. I *need* to talk to him." A pause. "He's one of us."

Noble shook his head. "He's one of our kind, but he's not one of us. You, me, Harlan, and Tora . . . we're a pack.

We belong together. Phelan is a lone wolf. If he wanted to be a part of anything, he would have done it a long time ago."

Argus shrugged his massive shoulders. "I still want to spend some time with him. I want to learn from him." A pause. "I might even want to join him in the woods."

Noble said nothing in response.

The call of the wild wasn't just some book you studied in school, it was a very real thing among members of the pack. Even Noble had felt it from time to time, and if that were true, then Argus must be feeling the call far stronger than any of them could imagine.

What to do? thought Noble. He couldn't fight Argus or force him to do something he didn't want to do. Any words about why the pack needed to stick together would only come across sounding like a lecture – and a lecture from a brother who was quite possibly younger than Argus by at least a minute or two. No, there was nothing he could do except let Argus find his own way, figure things out for himself.

Tora and Harlan had backtracked and were waiting for them on the path. "Are you two coming or not?" Harlan said.

Noble turned to Argus and smiled. "Say hello to Phelan for me."

"Sure."

"See you at school later?" Noble had managed to make it sound like a question.

"Maybe."

Tora took a few steps toward Noble on the path. "What's the matter with him?"

"Nothing," said Noble. "There's just something he needs to do."

"Like what?" asked Tora.

Noble ignored his sister and started for home without a word. Tora and Harlan followed, still wanting answers, but obviously willing to wait for them.

Argus remained where he was. Alone.

By the time they got home it was early morning. Ranger Brock was awake, sitting at the kitchen table, sipping hot chocolate and reading a recent edition of the *Prince George Citizen*.

Noble read the front-page headline; *Angry Spirits Turn Logging Site Upside Down*, and cracked a smile. There was a large picture of the two overturned vehicles and a smaller picture of Willie Greene set into it. Noble couldn't see all of the cutline, but he spied the word *Manchoka* under Willie's picture.

"Late night," said the ranger.

Noble shrugged. "Angry spirits work best in the dark."

The ranger said nothing for several moments. He had likely suspected that the pack had something to do with the strange goings on at the logging site, and now those suspicions were confirmed. "True," he said at last, "but they still need to be rested for school in the morning."

"We know," said Harlan from the hallway, already heading to bed.

The ranger looked around. "Where's Argus?"

Noble felt trapped. There were two options, neither of which he was happy with. He could either lie and tell the ranger that Argus wanted to run some more and had stayed out late to do it, or he could tell the truth and break the man's heart.

Tora and Harlan appeared in the doorway to the kitchen.

"It's okay," Noble told them. "You two go on to bed. I'll let the ranger know what happened."

"What? What happened?" Ranger Brock asked.

Noble took a seat at the kitchen table. "I know Willie's been talking about angry spirits and it all sounds kind of silly, but the land the company wants to harvest actually does have a special creature living on it."

"What kind of special creature?"

Noble sighed. "One of us," he said. "One of our kind."

The ranger's face went white. He swallowed as if his throat had suddenly gone dry. "Another member of your pack?"

Noble shook his head. "Yes and no. He's a full-grown male. His name is Phelan."

The ranger took a deep breath and finished his drink in a single gulp. He put the mug down on the table, nodding. "I suspected there were others. I mean, if you were out there how could there not be more?"

"He is like us, but not like us. He's big, strong, and wild. And he's spent all of his life in the woods, living off the land and doing his best to avoid contact with humans."

"So he let you find him?"

"Y-yes," Noble stammered. "I guess so. He said he knew our parents. He told us stories about them that made us proud."

The ranger was silent for a long, long time, struggling to keep his emotions in check. Finally, he took a deep breath and said, "Argus has gone to join him?"

"How did you know?"

"I knew it would come one day."

"You did?"

"Of course. You four are between worlds." He glanced in the direction of the master bedroom where Phyllis lay sleeping. "We've raised you as humans, but there are two parts to each of you, and it was only a matter of time before you would have to choose between them." The ranger shrugged and a tear leaked from the corner of his eye. "I just didn't think it would come so soon . . . or hurt so much."

Noble hated to see the ranger in so much pain. "Well, *I* don't want to go anywhere," he said.

The ranger smiled weakly. "You say that now, but give it time."

"Do you think Argus will be coming back?" The question came from Tora.

"I don't know," said the ranger. "I hope so, but it's his decision to make and he needs to make it on his own. The best we can do for him is support whatever it is he decides."

Harlan extended his hands, palms up as if there were a dozen questions left unanswered. "But how are we going to explain his disappearance? You can't just tell people he's gone. There'll be an investigation . . . and search parties and . . ."

"That'll be my problem when the time comes. Right now, you three have got to get some sleep. And I . . ." The ranger sighed and his body shuddered slightly. "I've got to break the news to Phyllis."

Noble wanted to help the ranger, but there was nothing he could do. "Good night," he said.

"Night," said Tora.

"See you later," Harlan chimed in.

"Good night," said the ranger, getting up from his chair. He followed the others down the hall, walking slowly, as if he were putting off telling Phyllis for as long as he could.

Chapter 15

The forest was hazy as the air, warmed by the early morning sun, clashed with the cool, moist forest floor. Argus slipped between the trees in his wolfen form, causing the mist to swirl and spiral around him as he ran. He was in the area where he'd seen Phelan twice before, but there was no sign of him anywhere; not on the ground or in the trees. If Harlan had been with him, the smaller wolf might have been able to pick up Phelan's scent, but Argus lacked Harlan's tracking abilities. As a result, he walked almost blindly in circles hoping he'd run into Phelan before he became too tired to continue.

Just then, a twig snapped in the distance. Argus looked in the direction of the sound and began moving slowly toward it.

And that's when he was pushed from behind. Argus plowed forward and over on his side, his left front paw gouging a deep line in the earth. As he looked behind him, he saw Phelan's towering figure standing over him, laughing.

"Didn't you hear me coming?" he asked in his familiar gruff voice.

Argus shifted his shape enough to allow himself speech, then shook his head. "There was a sound over there," he said, pointing in the direction he'd been headed.

"A stone thrown through the trees," Phelan laughed. "What's the saying? *The oldest trick in a book.*"

Argus joined in the laugh and got to his feet.

"Where are the others?" asked Phelan.

"At school. I came here by myself."

"Oh," Phelan said, almost in a grunt. "Why?"

Argus hesitated. He knew what he wanted, but he'd never been very good with words because he'd never had to be. Noble had always been the spokesman. Now that Argus had to express himself, he was at a loss for words. "I uh, I came here because I . . ." He paused, feeling his heart begin to pound and his body become hot all over. He knew he'd never be able to make it sound as good as Noble could, so he took a deep breath and just blurted it: "I want to join you and live in the forest, like my father did."

Phelan's eyes opened wide and his head jerked back as if Argus had taken a swing at him. He quickly recovered and shook his head. "No. No, no . . . . No, you can't."

"What? Why not?"

"No. It's not a good idea."

"But I'm big and strong, and I'm a good fighter. If I lived in the wild, I could be alpha male of a pack."

"Is that why you want to leave your brothers and sister? To be alpha male of a pack – *if* you find one and *if* they allow you to join them in the first place?"

It was Argus's turn to be taken aback. Obviously there were many things he had yet to consider.

"I *allowed* you to find me," Phelan continued. "Our kind – those of us who were born and raised in the wild – are excellent at hiding from our enemies . . . and anyone else we don't want finding us. You and your brothers have barely come of age, and you've already allowed one of your kind to be trapped by a human, *and* your images to be captured on one of their machines."

Phelan was referring to Doctor Edward Monk, who'd videotaped the pack changing shape in the forest before he kidnapped Tora in an attempt to take her out of the woods. How Phelan knew about that adventure was curious, but he obviously knew more about them than he'd let on.

Argus didn't know what to say in the pack's defence. It was true they'd nearly allowed themselves to be revealed to the rest of the world, but they'd learned from their mistakes. Besides, there were many instances where their kind had been seen by humans. "What about the Sasquatch legends – Bigfoot and all that?"

A smile crossed Phelan's face. "That was our creation, a way to explain those rare times when one of our kind is careless and is seen by humans. It has worked too. So many sightings, and still no proof."

That was true enough, but Argus wasn't about to turn around and head back home with his tail between his legs. "I'm here now, though. And I want to live in the wild. I can learn from you. I can become like you." He paused. "Please!"

Phelan's hand came out of nowhere and struck Argus hard on the cheek, knocking him to the ground. "You can never be like me!" he said, his voice rough and angry. "It's too late for you."

Argus rubbed his cheek with his hand, and felt several loose teeth with his tongue. It had felt wrong to plead with Phelan and the werewolf had made him pay for it. Argus was utterly confused and on the verge of tears.

Phelan continued, but his voice was soft now, almost apologetic. "Even if you could become like me, I would not want you to. I want you to stay where you are, with your pack."

"But that's not what *I* want."

"No. living in the forest is what you *think* you want. Believe me, living wild is harder than anything you can imagine. Sure, it's nice to run through the woods, kill something and gorge on its blood, but what would you do in the winter when the snow is piled waist deep and the only thing to eat is tree bark and dead bears."

Argus wrinkled his nose at the thought of eating the rotten carcass of a bear.

"You see, our kind is slowly dying off because the world we live in is getting smaller each year. But you and your pack can help us preserve our way of life and grow strong again."

"How can we do that?" Argus asked, feeling better the longer they talked.

"By living among humans and working to safeguard our kind from within their world."

Argus thought about that a moment. They were trying to save the forest north of Redstone from the logging company in ways that Phelan could never have dreamed of. Their efforts were paying off, and people were saying that it was only a matter of time before the company pulled up their stakes and moved on. Maybe there was something to what Phelan was saying.

"If you continue to live with humans you will become the strongest and most powerful beings our kind has ever known." He paused a moment to let it sink in, then said. "Do you understand?"

Argus nodded. He did understand a little. They were already working to rescue Phelan's forest from harvest, but that was such a small thing. Imagine what the pack might be able to accomplish if Noble became a member of British Columbia's parliament, or even provincial premier. And what if Harlan became a computer whiz, or a scientist who used his skills to teach humankind about conservation? And Tora, she had the looks and talent to be a television personality, a journalist who specialized in environmental issues. And what of Argus himself? He loved the forests and the wild, he could easily end up being a ranger just like Ranger Brock.

Not like his father . . . but like his adoptive father.

Suddenly, Argus felt silly for venturing out into the forest in pursuit of some wild idea about living in the woods. He would be lost out there on his own, especially after he'd been raised in the comfort of the Brocks' world.

"I do understand," he said at last.

"Good. Then go back to your pack and use the human world to help your kind survive."

Argus nodded. "I will, but . . ."

"Yes?"

"Can we come back and visit?"

"Anytime."

"Where will we find you?"

"Just look for me, and I will find you." He turned then, and bounded off into the forest. Argus watched him for several moments and then lost him between the trees. Gone.

With a sigh, Argus turned and started walking.

It was a long trek through the woods, and it seemed even longer after his meeting with Phelan, but when he arrived at Ranger Brock's house at least he'd know he was home.

Where he belonged.

"I'm outta here," said Bill Droine, jamming his clothes into a duffel bag. His face was white and his hands trembled noticeably as he gathered together his belongings. He'd been working for the company for more than ten years and his bailing out didn't bode well for the fate of the project. There were four other men standing around inside the trailer and it looked as if at least two of them were contemplating doing the same thing.

"It couldn't have been that bad," said Grant Willem, number two man on the site, who'd worked with Droine on countless logging operations. But unlike Droine, Willem was a big man – well over three hundred pounds – who had slept like, well, like a log, through the night and had missed all of the excitement.

"Are you kiddin' me?" Droine said, picking up his toothbrush, shaver, and comb and tossing them into his travel bag. "It's one thing for that crazy Manchoka to be talkin' about angry spirits, but it's a whole other thing to be staring up at a hairy seven-foot beast that's got claws the length of my fingers and teeth sharper than a ripsaw."

"You got to get off the bottle," Willem said. "There hasn't been a Bigfoot sighting around here in years."

The rest of the men in the trailer laughed.

Droine glared at them with contempt, knowing full well that they'd all been just as afraid as he had been, and were putting up a brave face only now because Willem was teasing him.

"Laugh all you want, big man," Droine said, "but you've got a wife, right?"

Willem nodded.

"Well, you think about her living out the rest of her days on her own because you decided to make jokes about something that's dead serious."

The laughter stopped.

Just then the door sprang open and Tyler Allen Ceballo burst into the trailer. "What the hell do you think you're doing?" he fumed, spit flying from his lips along with the words.

"Leaving!" said Droine. "I'm gettin' out while I still can."

"You're not going anywhere." The words were a statement, as if it were a fact that could not be challenged or argued no matter what the reasoning.

"The hell you say!" shouted Droine. "I don't know what those things are, but they're nothing human, that's for damn sure. I stared one down, face to face. It had different colored eyes, the smell of blood on its breath, and one of its hands went all the way around my neck. It could have killed me if it had wanted to, and if we stay here any longer it's going to want to. Guaranteed."

The loggers who'd been thinking of leaving with Droine seemed to be leaning toward the door. Droine had been one of the best in the crew for years, and if he'd been spooked, there was definitely something out there to be afraid of, even if it wasn't exactly the way he described it.

"They're just messing with us," Ceballo said, his voice straddling the line between comfort and pleading. "They've got some Native spouting off about angry spirits. He's good, I gotta give him that, but he's an actor, for crying out loud. Then they get some of the locals to put on fur suits and run around like they're 'angry spirits'." He was smiling now, as if the whole thing was some big joke. "I mean, c'mon, we've been through this sort of thing before. It's a battle of public opinion. People get angry at first, but once we spread a little money around, and talk about jobs, they always come around."

Droine looked unconvinced.

"Locals in fur suits for crying out loud! C'mon men, we don't scare that easily."

"Speak for yourself," Droine said.

"Hey, nobody's been hurt." It was a statement, but somehow there was an air of desperation to it, as if Ceballo knew he was losing ground and was pulling out all the stops to convince his men to stay.

"Yet!" said Droine. "This one isn't like the others. There's something on this land that people are willing to go to an awful lot of trouble to protect, and it's only a matter of time before someone get's hurt. *Bad*." He glared at Ceballo. "It might even be you."

"If you leave now, Droine, you can't come back," Ceballo said.

"There are other sites. The company's got plenty of work right now."

Ceballo shook his head. "No, it's not going to work like that. You leave now, you're gone. Out! Fired!"

Droine looked unsure. Ceballo might be bluffing.

"And I'll make certain you don't work for anyone else, either," he continued. "No one's going to want a yellow-bellied tree-hugger on their crew. You work for me now, or you don't work. Period!" He looked around the room. "And that goes for the rest of you."

"At least I'll still be alive to walk to the unemployment line," Droine said under his breath. He left the trailer, slamming the door behind him.

Ceballo stepped in front of the door to block the way. "Anyone else?"

The rest of the men were too afraid to speak up. They still might leave, but if they did, they'd do it later, when Ceballo wasn't looking.

"All right, then," he said. "Let's get to work and show these people they don't scare us one bit."

But the men were scared . . . as much of Ceballo as they were of the spirits that haunted the forest each night.

Chapter 16

They could hear the school bus coming down the road toward them. There was a plume of dust rising up between the trees, and the thrum of its diesel engine was growing louder by the second.

Argus was nowhere in sight.

"He's not going to show, is he?" Harlan asked.

Noble shrugged. "I don't know."

Tora took a quick look around. "Do you think he's gone forever?"

Again Noble shrugged. "I don't know."

"Why would he want to leave, anyway?" Harlan asked. "There are four of us. We've always been *four*, and we always will be *four*. We're stuck with each other for life, whether we like it or not."

Noble looked at his smaller brother and smiled. "You say that now, but things change, no matter how much you don't want them to."

Tora said nothing, and judging by the look on her face, she knew and understood what Noble was saying. She was in love, or at least in *like* with Michael. One day she might want to spend more time with him, and who knows, even get married. When that happened, she'd have to tell him of their secret and they'd no longer be four, but five. Harlan too might find someone, or decide he'd like to pursue a career in computers that would take him out of the forest and into the city – Vancouver, Toronto, maybe Waterloo. Tora had expressed interest in perhaps becoming a vet or an actress, and either choice would require schooling. And what about himself? He might want to become a doctor or a lawyer or maybe even a politician. One thing was for certain, in a few years the pack would be scattered to the four winds with faint hope of regrouping and settling back into the forest from which they'd come. So much could happen over the years that they all had to be prepared for change. They had to adapt to it, not resist it.

But instead of explaining all that to Harlan and sounding like he was giving a sermon, Noble simply said, "We'll always be a pack. Argus just has to find his way."

The bus had crested the last rise in the roadway and was now bearing down on them. They'd be on it in minutes.

"Hey!" a voice cried from the end of the drive near the house.

They all turned to see Argus running toward them.

"Like I said," Harlan commented smugly. "We are four. Always have been. Always will be."

"Good to see you," Noble said as Argus arrived. "We were wondering if you'd ever be coming back."

Argus was all smiles, but his grin seemed strained somehow, as if he were putting on a brave face. "Are you kiddin' me? I wouldn't leave you guys for anything. I just needed, well, some time to think, you know."

"Did you talk to Phelan?"

"I did."

"And what did you learn?"

"That he's a little too wild for my liking."

That much was true, Noble thought. Even though Phelan was probably closer to what their real parents had been like, he was too far removed from what they'd become to be thought of as family. But that was his opinion, Argus had to make his own decisions and come to his own realizations. Of course, Phelan might not have wanted Argus hanging around . . . In the end, Noble decided that it didn't matter what had happened in the forest. Argus had returned to them and that was all that was important.

"Besides," Argus said, making light of the situation to save face with his brothers and sister. "We're a team. And no matter how disappointing it might seem, you guys are stuck with me for life, so you better get used to it."

Tora was the first one to step forward. "I'm not disappointed," she said, putting her arms around him and giving him a hug. "I'm glad."

Harlan welcomed his brother back into the pack.

The bus pulled to a stop and the doors opened.

Noble joined in with the rest. It felt good to be together.

"Uh, I hate to break up this feel-good moment," said the bus driver, "but I have a schedule to keep."

The pack separated and stepped onto the bus without another word.

At school Tora left her brothers and hurried off on her own. Michael Martin had gotten a ride from his father and was waiting for her in the library. She put her things in her locker, took what she needed for the morning classes, and hurried off to meet him.

Michael was sitting at a table in the corner with the play book open in front of him.

"The bus just arrived," she said. "Have you been here long?"

He shook his head. "Twenty minutes. Maybe less."

"Sorry."

"We could've given you a ride. My dad told me it wouldn't be a problem."

"No, that's okay. It wouldn't have felt right, leaving my brothers behind."

Michael nodded.

"What scene do you want to rehearse?" she asked.

"The opening," he said. "I practiced last night in front of the mirror and I think I sound a little older now."

Tora smiled. She wasn't quite sure how rehearsing in front of a *mirror* was supposed to make you *sound* older, but she was thrilled Michael was trying hard to make this work. He wasn't an especially good actor, but he was making an effort for her and that was something special.

She began the opening scene.

As Michael read from the book, he did manage to make his voice sound a bit older.

By the time they were halfway through the scene, it was obvious that they were improving.

And then the library door opened to reveal Maria Abruzzo standing in the doorway, a sly grin on her face.

Michael read until Maria's laughter caught his attention.

"Something funny, Maria?"

"You two are still rehearsing," she said with an incredulous tone to her voice.

"Of course we are," said Michael. "The auditions are on Monday."

Maria stepped into the library and slowly made her way toward their table. "Oh, so I guess you haven't heard."

"Heard what?" Tora wanted to know.

The grin on Maria's face grew into a wicked smile. "My father's trucking company is sponsoring the drama festival."

"What?" Michael gasped.

Tora's heart sank into the pit of her stomach.

"That's a conflict of interest," Michael said. "You can't be in the play if your father's putting up the money for it."

"Take it up with Principal Terashita," she said. "He seemed pretty happy to get his hands on the check and assured my father the production would be much better now that they had the money for props and costumes."

"That's not fair!" was all Tora could manage.

"Fair?" she laughed. "You want to be an actress and you haven't the slightest idea how the system works."

"You mean the audition?"

"No, show business, stupid. Money's put up all the time to make sure the right people get the right parts. It happens in Hollywood every day."

"Redstone isn't Hollywood Maria," Michael said.

"Maybe, but it's done all over the world. My father put up the money and Principal Terashita took it." She stood there smiling for the longest time as if there wasn't anything more to be said. Then she twirled around on her heels and walked out of the library.

Tora groaned and slumped down onto the table. "I'll never get this part now."

Michael's eyes swept back and forth over the table, as if there was an answer hidden there that he just couldn't see. "Oh yes, you will."

"Her father's putting up the money for the show. That basically makes him the producer. Mr. Terashita's taken the money, so it won't be too hard for him to have Maria "win" the audition for the part. I'll be lucky if I even get on stage. I'll end up assistant prop master, or lighting director. You just wait and see."

Michael said nothing. Everything Tora said was true and there was really no counter to it. Tora wouldn't get the part she wanted, and if Maria Abruzzo was feeling especially mean, she'd probably be able to arrange it so that Tora wasn't even part of the show. But the look on Michael's face suggested he wasn't about to give in so easily. "You keep rehearsing the part and who knows what could happen."

Tora lifted her head. "Yeah, like what?"

Michael shrugged. "I don't know. Maybe you'll just be so much better than her that they'll have to give you the part. Or maybe if a better part comes up . . . or a different part, yeah, Maria will want it instead."

"Those things aren't going to happen and you know it."

"Maybe she'll get sick and you'll have to step in at the last minute and save the show."

Tora considered it. She had to admit, it sounded good. "How's she going to get sick?"

"I don't know. But I bet it could be arranged."

"No! I don't want to get the part like that."

"Okay," Michael said, pausing to think. "Maybe we could ask Noble. He's good with plans. I bet he could come up with something."

Tora shook her head. "I don't need Noble's help every time something goes wrong." Saying the words made her feel better, if only slightly. "I'm going to get that part because I'm better for it than Maria is, and if I don't, then I'll be so good in the audition that everyone in school will *know* she only won out because of her father's money."

There was a smile on Michael's face. "That's the spirit!"

Tora took a deep breath and let out a long sigh that did wonders to strengthen her resolve. "Let's get back to rehearsing," she said. "I've got to nail this role so there's no doubt that I'm the best one for it."

"I'm convinced already," said Michael.

Tora smiled.

Chapter 17

Word traveled pretty quickly. Harlan and Jake MacKinnon were meeting after school to sort out their differences – without any interference from family, friends, and most of all, teachers. How news of the fight never made its way to Principal Terashita or any of the staff was a mystery. Perhaps the principal had been too busy with the drama auditions to keep up with what was going on *inside* the school, but that didn't account for the teachers. Noble had an idea that the staff were well aware of Jake's bullying and figured this was the day he would get what was coming to him. That was all well and good, but part of Noble's plan was to have the confrontation stopped before it happened, demonstrating that Harlan was willing to fight for himself without there having to be any actual violence.

But it was a couple of minutes to four and although there were at least thirty or more students filing into the hallway at the rear of the school, there still wasn't a teacher in sight.

Noble and Harlan stood in the hallway just outside the boys' change room, waiting for Argus. Argus emerged a minute later with a sly smile on his face.

"Is it all set?" Noble asked.

Argus said nothing, choosing instead to show Noble the two lengths of wire he'd removed from the change room's light switches.

"Good," Noble said.

Argus slipped the wires into his jacket pocket.

Just then Jake and his toadies entered the school through the rear doors. There were six of them altogether and they all looked as if they were ready to fight their friend's battle for him.

"So you decided to show, huh?" MacKinnon said, gesturing to Harlan with a flick of his head while he kept his hands deep inside his pockets. "I thought a dog like you would have run off with your tail between your legs."

Harlan shook his head with a smile. "I wouldn't miss this for anything." He knew what was in store, and was more confident because of it.

Jake looked over at Noble. "So what do you have in mind? You gonna let me fight your little brother, or what?"

Noble ignored the "little brother" comment. Harlan was often mistaken for a little brother because he was so much smaller than the others. Harlan, however, was angered by the comment, and would use that rage to his advantage.

"Be my guest," Noble said.

"Then let's step outside."

Nobel shook his head. "No, not outside."

"Where then?"

"In there." Noble pointed to the change room. "Two of you go in, the last one out is the winner."

Jake smiled. Obviously the thought of an enclosed space appealed to him. "Nobody else inside, right?"

"That's right."

"Then let's do it!" Jake seemed eager to get inside the change room.

"Hold on!" said Argus, blocking the doorway. "What's in your pocket?"

"What?" he said. "Nothing!"

"Mind if I check?"

Jake was about to protest, but Argus didn't bother waiting to hear what he had to say. He patted down Jake's jacket and discovered a knife that sported a four-inch blade in one of his pockets.

There was a low rumble from the crowd of students, as they suddenly realized that, aside from being a bully, Jake MacKinnon was a very dangerous individual, and quite possibly crazy.

"Your idea of a fair fight, MacKinnon?"

Jake looked as if he'd just been caught with his pants down around his ankles. "I forgot that was in there."

Argus nodded, unconvinced. "Sure you did."

"It's not even my knife," he said. "I'm holding it for a friend of mine."

Noble just shook his head. "Any more of your *friend's* stuff on you?"

Argus continued to search Jake's clothes. When he was done he looked up at Noble and said, "That's it!"

"Hey," one of Jake's friends cried, pointing at Harlan. "I want to check *him*."

"Go ahead," Harlan said, putting his hands up against the wall.

"Nothing," said Jake's pal, patting Harlan down.

"All right then," Noble said. "Go ahead."

Harlan looked at Noble and Argus, nodded once, then slipped inside the change room. Jake followed.

"Hey, it's dark in here," Jake said.

The change room had no windows and with the two light switches disabled, the room was pitch-black even in the middle of the day. Darkness would make both boys virtually blind, but Harlan's keen sense of smell would enable him to know where Jake was at all times. Best of all, because Jake wouldn't be able to see, Harlan was free to adopt any shape he wanted for the fight, and he would be able to deal with Jake in short order.

The crowd in the hallway was silent for the first few seconds, anxious to hear any sound – good or bad – coming from inside the change room. The silence was broken half a minute later when someone screamed, "Hey! Ow!"

Jake's crew laughed at that, exchanging high fives and slapping each other on the back.

The rest of the crowd slowly followed suit as more and more cries for help emanated from the room.

Argus and Noble however, remained steadfast, not letting even a hint of emotion cross their faces.

"Stop it, please!" someone shouted in a high-pitched voice that was so amplified by the tiled walls of the change room that it was hard to tell whose it was. The cry was followed by a slap and a loud tearing sound.

And then . . . silence.

The crowd in the hallway held their collective breath as they waited for someone to emerge.

Who would it be?

Jake's crew acted as if they knew.

But so did Noble and Argus.

Steps approached the door. One . . . two . . . and the door slowly opened to reveal Jake wobbling on two rubbery legs. There was a welt growing under his left eye, a bruise on his right cheek, and he was hugging his torso like a couple of ribs had been broken.

The crowd gasped.

Jake's buddies were speechless for a moment, until one of them said, "First or last out of the room, it don't matter. Let's see what the other one looks like."

The door swung open a moment later to reveal Harlan standing there without a scratch on him. His hair looked a little disheveled and his clothes were a bit out of place, but other than that he looked just as good as when he'd stepped into the room. He straightened his jacket, looked over at Jake's gang, and said, "If any of you want some of that, you know where to find me!"

Noble shook Harlan's hand and patted his brother on the back. "Good job. There isn't a cut on him," he said, referring to the danger of wounding MacKinnon and turning the bully into one of them.

"No," said Harlan. "I was careful."

Argus gave his brother a hug. "You did good."

Noble gathered Argus and Harlan together and said, "We'll celebrate later. Right now, we've got to get out of here."

They hurried out through the rear doors of the school.

Behind them they could hear Principal Terashita coming down the hallway. "What's going on here?" he asked. Then, "Jake MacKinnon. I might have known. What happened? Pick on the wrong person this time? This was bound to happen . . ."

The principal kept on talking, and the longer he did, the more it sounded like justice.

Chapter 18

The protesters outnumbered the loggers four to one now, and it was obvious to everyone in the area that Conservco wasn't going to win this fight. Donna Hughson's efforts had been seriously underestimated by the company and her band of seemingly harmless old ladies had thrown up a wall of protest that captured the attention of the nation. Spearheaded by members of the Writers' Union of Canada, articles appeared in every major magazine and newspaper in the country. *Maclean's* did a cover story on the protest, and the *National Post*, *The Globe and Mail*, even the *Toronto Star* ran feature articles in their Saturday editions. There had been several television reporters on site since the second day of the protest, and they'd fed the networks raw footage and news reports all week long.

Despite the increased numbers and all the attention, the pack didn't have much trouble sneaking into camp. There were more armed men posted to guard the campsite, but they tended to stick together for safety and, as a result, the holes between them were larger than before. But the pack weren't interested in the men working *on* the site this time around. They had scared away most of them and it had become apparent that the only real obstacle left was the boss, Tyler Allen Ceballo. According to the loggers who'd jumped ship, he was a nasty, manipulating, devil of a man who was determined to win the battle at all cost. So far, he'd been pretty easygoing about the safety of his men, and the pack wanted to know how much of a *personal* sacrifice he was willing to make for the sake of the company.

"It's this one," Harlan said, leaning up against the side of Ceballo's trailer in his werewolf form and sniffing around the doorframe. "He's in there."

Noble nodded. "You stay out here with Tora," he said. "Anyone comes by, you scare them off."

Harlan nodded, as did his sister.

Noble turned to Argus. "You sure you want to do this?"

Argus smiled. "Are you kidding? I can't wait."

The plan was simple. They'd done a good job of scaring off the workers, but Ceballo was still the man in charge. He'd dismissed everything that had happened as simple trickery and "men in fur suits." The time had come to convince the boss – personally – that it was in his best interest to move his operation a little farther north.

The door to the trailer opened with a sharp squeak. Noble held it still for a moment, but it was impossible to open it any further without making more noise. Finally, Noble shrugged and pulled the door wide open.

The squeak cut through the night air, but Ceballo didn't wake up immediately. Instead, he snorted and *harrumphed* a couple of times.

"Who . . . what?"

There were no lights on inside of the trailer, but there were lights on outside in the camp that cast patches of light on the walls and floor. Noble and Argus used the shadows to their advantage, allowing Ceballo only fleeting glimpses of their faces and bodies as they moved through the trailer.

"Who's there? Is that you Willem?"

Noble and Argus approached the cot where Ceballo still lay, half-awake, half-asleep.

Noble took a position at the end of the bed, so that only the left side of his wolfen face was caught by the light. Argus stepped up to the side of the bed, his head and legs in shadow, but his muscular chest fully illuminated by the outside lights. Noble kicked one of the bed's legs.

"What the . . ." Ceballo sat up in bed. "Who the hell are you?"

"Get out!" Noble said, doing his best to say the words in a menacing, guttural growl.

"I'm not going –"

Ceballo managed just three words before Argus punched

him in the side of the head. The blow knocked the man out cold and he flopped back down on the bed.

"Easy, easy," Noble said.

"I didn't hit him *that* hard."

"And don't use your hand," Noble instructed. "If you break the skin and he gets infected –"

"I know, I know."

They looked around the trailer.

"Here!" said Noble, handing Argus an ax handle. "Try this."

Argus felt the wooden handle in his hand, swinging it several times to find the right balance.

Ceballo's eyes fluttered open. "I'm not . . . We're not leaving. You can't scare –"

Argus hit Ceballo with the handle and he immediately blacked out.

"Works like a charm," Argus said, hefting the ax handle in his hand.

"Good," said Noble. "Let's go."

Argus reached down and picked Ceballo up off the bed. With hardly any effort, the huge werewolf threw the man over his left shoulder and carried him out of the trailer.

"Anyone around?" Noble asked Tora.

She shook her head.

"What did you hit him with?" Harlan wanted to know. "It sounded like a home run."

Argus carried Ceballo from the camp to a large redwood that was about twenty-five meters away. The tree rose up more than a hundred feet in the air with branches up top that were more than thick enough for what the pack had in mind.

"Can you do it?" Noble asked Argus, as they stood at the base of the tree.

Harlan and Tora were busy wrapping a length of rope around Argus's waist. When they were done, Argus twisted left and right, bent his knees and adjusted the unconscious Ceballo over his shoulder. "No problem," he said. "But I'll need my hand free."

Noble thought about it for a moment, then took the ax handle from him.

At that point, Ceballo roused once more, mumbling a string of words. "We're harvesting these trees whether you like it or –"

Argus took a step forward, slamming Ceballo's head into the massive trunk of the redwood. Again, the man was out like a light. "How careless of me," Argus said, smiling.

"Okay then," Noble said. He stepped back from the tree along with Harlan and Tora.

They watched Argus begin climbing.

Grant Willem stepped around another trailer, looked left and right, then scratched his head. The man was just nowhere to be seen. He tried another trailer, checking both the inside and out, even underneath – just in case the man had had a bit too much to drink and had decided to slip beneath the trailer to sleep it off.

Not that Tyler Allen Ceballo was much of a drinker. He liked the odd beer with the boys after a long, hard day's work, but he'd never been drunk, let alone hungover. Mind you, the past few days had been pretty tough on him, supervising a logging operation that few people wanted in the first place, and even fewer wanted as the days passed. It was conceivable that the stress had gotten to him and he'd done something stupid. Even so, it wasn't like the man to just up and leave without telling someone where he was going.

"Have you seen him?" Brian McAteer asked as he met up with Willem in the middle of the site. Most of the men were still asleep, retiring from their guard posts once the sun had come up half an hour ago.

"Not a sign of him," Willem said. "It's like he just . . . well, vanished into thin air."

McAteer shook his head. "It isn't like him, that's for sure."

At this time in the morning, Ceballo was usually in the office trailer sipping his second cup of coffee and figuring out strategies to win over public support. It had become increasingly difficult and Ceballo had reacted by being even harder on the few men who had stuck with him. According to those who'd been with the company for a few years, Ceballo had never lost one of these battles, and the possibility of losing this one was weighing heavily on his shoulders.

"Where do you think he could be?" Willem asked.

McAteer shrugged and shook his head. "Beats me."

Willem removed his Vancouver Canucks ball cap and drew a sleeve across his forehead. He'd been up and down the side of the mountain twice this morning and he was hot, sweaty, and tired. He was looking forward to seeing this standoff resolved – one way or another – so he could go home and spend some time with his family.

"Maybe he went for a walk. It looks like it's going to be a nice day."

Willem glanced up at the sun, which was minutes from clearing the tops of the trees to the east, and saw a strange shape among the branches. "What the –"

"What is it?"

The trees in this part of the forest were sometimes home to predatory birds that built massive nests in the upper branches. Those nests could sometimes be seen from the ground if the angle was right and the sun was in the correct position. But even birds' nests couldn't explain the size of that solid lump that was sitting up in a tree a short distance down the road. If it were a nest, the bird would have to be the size of a large dog.

"Do you see that?" Willem said, pointing at the nest-shaped object up in the trees.

"No," McAteer said at first. Then, "Yeah, okay, I see it now."

"What do you think it is?"

"I don't know."

"Could it be –"

Just then the object moved, slowly at first, then abruptly, as if it were about to fall out of the tree.

"Holy cow!" said McAteer.

"How the hell did he get up there?"

The question went unanswered as the two men started running down the road toward the tree.

He could feel the breeze blow through his hair. But it was also blowing through his clothes, and his legs and feet were cold. The usually comfortable feeling he felt each morning was absent, as if instead of a bed, he were lying on top of a woodpile with branches and pine needles sticking into his body from head to toe.

And his head.

Lord, did it hurt.

His head felt like it had been dealt a half-dozen hammer blows. But how could that be? He tried to remember back to the night before. It was hazy, but there was some recollection of the beasts. Yes, there had been creatures. Hairy things that had come to him in the night and spirited him out of his trailer and away.

Impossible. It couldn't have been real. Perhaps a dream. Yeah, that was it. A dream, a nightmare. Yes, with monstrous creatures . . . all conjured up in his mind because of the stress and pressure he'd been under the past few days.

The wind picked up and he could feel himself being rocked, almost like a child in a cradle, or an adult in a hammock. But then something cracked and his body dropped several inches.

Ceballo opened one eye.

I must still be dreaming, he thought. *How else would I be hundreds of feet off the ground and tied to a tree?*

A pause for a moment of thought.

Hundreds of feet off the ground?

He opened his other eye and glanced around. *Trees. That's odd.* And then he turned his head slightly and looked down. The ground was so far away.

Just then a piece of branch broke free and he watched as it fell, bouncing off other limbs, tumbling and drifting down to the ground, where more than a dozen people stood, gazing up at him. Some of them had cameras for photographs and television.

What on earth had happened last night? In the dream the creatures had spirited him away. *Now that was an odd choice of words.* Spirited. *Could it be that the Indian was telling the truth? Had the spirits he'd talked about taken him from his bed and put him up in the trees as a warning?*

The wind rocked him again, the sound of the breeze was punctuated by the sound of snapping wood.

"Help!" he gasped, but the word was carried away on the wind. He tried again, this time grabbing hold of the trunk, or at least what was left of it at this height, and took a deep breath. "Help me!" he screamed. "Help me get down from here!"

There was movement on the ground, and voices shouting: "Hold on!" and "Hang in there!"

Tyler Allen Ceballo did as they instructed, tightening his grip on the tree and vowing not to let go until he knew he was safe.

And while he waited, he made a promise . . . to himself, and maybe even to God. "If I make it down alive," he whispered, "my next job will be in an office, sitting behind a desk made of plastic and steel."

It took four hours, but the logging crew eventually managed to lower Tyler Allen Ceballo back down to earth, alive. Although he was strapped into a basket, when he reached the ground it was obvious that he was trembling. It was possible he was cold, but there was the distinct look of fear in his eyes, as if he'd seen a ghost . . . or even an angry spirit.

"I'm out of here," he mumbled.

"What?" asked Willem.

"What'd he say?" echoed Brian McAteer.

"He said he's out of here," a nearby protester answered.

"He wants to go home . . ." someone else said.

". . . to his mama," added another.

A round of laughter coursed through the crowd.

Willem got down on his knees and leaned forward so his ear was close to Ceballo's mouth and he could more clearly hear what the man had to say. "What did you say?" he asked.

"I'm . . ." Ceballo said, then swallowed. "I'm out of here."

"Yeah, we got you down. You're gonna be all right."

He shook his head. "No," he said. "I want out . . . of the forest. Too dangerous here."

Willem straightened up and looked around as if he were having trouble believing what he was hearing. It sounded like they were going to pull out of this site.

Ceballo took a deep breath. "There are monsters here!"

"Yeah," came a voice from the crowd. "And they work for Conservco."

"No," Ceballo shook his head. "There are creatures in the forest here."

"Don't you mean spirits?"

This time the voice didn't belong to a nameless, faceless protester. The words came from Willie Greene. Greene stepped forward until he towered over Ceballo, still strapped to the rescue basket.

"Monsters, creatures, spirits . . ." He shook his head again as if to rid himself of the nightmare images playing upon his mind. "Call them whatever you like. I don't know what the hell they were, I just want out."

"So you'll be moving on?" Willie's voice was calm, without a hint of emotion.

"I don't know what *they'll* be doing. All I know is, I'll be getting out of the lumber game."

A cheer erupted from the crowd. Even though the fate of the site was still up in the air, it was obvious that Tyler Allen Ceballo wasn't going to be in charge much longer. And with Ceballo gone, it was unlikely the company would have someone else ready to step in and do the company's dirty work for them.

In effect, the stand-off was over, thanks to the efforts of a group of tree-hugging, blue-haired old ladies, and the "angry spirits" called on by Willie Greene.

The loggers delivered Ceballo into the back of a company truck and slowly drove away. It was only a matter of time before the rest of the men and vehicles would be gone as well.

"Three cheers for Willie Greene!" someone shouted.

"Hip-hip, hurray!"

"Hip-hip, hurray!"

"Hip-hip, hurray!"

At the back of the crowd four teenagers cheered along with everyone else. But when the cheering ended and Willie Greene was carried off on the shoulders of two large men, the four remained where they were, continuing their own celebrations by discreetly shaking hands and giving one another a pat on the back that said, "Well done."

Chapter 19

There was an electric buzz coursing through school on Monday, but only in part because the logging company had decided to move their operation farther north over the weekend. The other big news was that Principal Terashita would be making a special announcement at the drama night auditions after school. Tora was beside herself with dread. She saw no reason why the surprise announcement would bring anything but disappointment. It was probably going to be something stupid like Maria Abruzzo's father was buying all the costumes, or paying for the whole production to compete in the high-school drama festival in Vancouver . . . anything to put his daughter in a brighter spotlight on a bigger stage.

"Thank you all for coming out this afternoon," said Principal Terashita.

There were at least two dozen students there, all vying for fewer than six lead roles, five if you gave one of them to Maria.

Tora sighed. All she'd wanted was a chance to prove herself. A fair chance.

Michael gave her arm a tender squeeze. "Relax," he said. "We're going to give it our best shot, and whatever happens, happens."

She nodded in response, but the gesture was just for Michael's sake. What she really wanted was to tear Maria apart and feed on her insides.

"Now I'm sure you're all wondering what my 'special surprise' is, and I won't make you wait much longer." He paused a moment, to clear his throat, then continued. "As you know, Mr. Enzo Abruzzo, owner of Abruzzo Trucking –"

"That's my dad!" Maria said.

"– Uh, yes, indeed, that is your father's company, Maria," the principal said. "Anyway, Mr. Abruzzo has agreed to sponsor our drama night and for that we're supremely grateful."

He began clapping his hands and everyone followed suit.

"And because of his generous donation, we were able to afford to hire a special drama coach to help us make this year's drama night our best one yet."

No applause this time, but the news certainly caused a stir.

"So it's with great pleasure that I introduce you to Redstone's most famous actor, Manchoka himself, Mr. Willie Greene!"

The door to the auditorium opened up and in walked Willie Greene dressed in a pair of casual pants, a beige suede jacket, and full wrap-around sunglasses – despite the dim auditorium lighting.

"Willie has just been cast to star in the new production of Mordecai Richler's *The Incomparable Atuck*."

Everyone in the room cheered and applauded.

"But before he heads off to Labrador for filming, Willie has agreed to help us out with our auditions by being our special guest judge . . ."

Tora's heart leapt up into her throat. *Could it be?*

". . . casting the roles in the plays however he sees fit."

"Yes!" Tora said aloud.

Several people stared at her for a moment, then turned their attention back to Principal Terashita.

"So good luck with the auditions everyone," he said. "I have a feeling this year's show is going to be our best one ever."

Tora couldn't believe her luck. She was going to have a fair chance at winning the role after all.

"That's pretty exciting, eh?" said Michael.

She nodded, and glanced around the room, noticing that everyone shared Michael's sense of excitement.

Everyone, that is, except for Maria Abruzzo, who looked as if her balloon had just popped.

"It's more than exciting," Tora said. "It's *fair!*"

Noble, Argus, and Harlan slipped into the auditorium, careful not to open the door too wide and let light flood into the room from the hallway.

Tora was onstage with Michael performing the final scene from the play, *Red Carnations*.

Argus jabbed an elbow into Noble's side. "There she is."

"Yeah," Noble said. "And Michael Martin."

Argus was silent for several moments. "She looks good."

Noble nodded. He found it hard to think of Tora as being cute, pretty, good-looking, or sexy. It was even harder to think of her like that when she could transform herself into a towering creature that was half-human, half-wolf, capable of tearing full-grown men apart with her bare hands. But Noble had to admit, Tora was developing into a very attractive young woman. He felt proud as he watched her up on stage making use of her newfound beauty. But more than good-looking, Tora was talented. Noble knew that she had a passion for acting, that she wanted to try it out and see if she was any good. Watching her up on stage made it clear that she was a natural. Her smile, body language, tone of voice, and speech all seemed *right*.

Michael, on the other hand, wasn't very good at all. His costume looked okay, and he said all the correct words when he was supposed to, but there was no feeling there.

Even though he had memorized his lines, he still sounded as if he were reading them off the page. Obviously Michael had rehearsed with Tora strictly because he knew she wanted a part in drama night. That thought put a smile on Noble's face. Michael obviously cared very much for his sister, and if he ended up being Tora's mate, the two of them would make a good pair.

The scene was coming to an end. The time had come for Tora and Michael to kiss.

Harlan giggled, knowing what was coming.

Argus gave his smaller brother a stiff punch on the arm and Harlan stopped laughing.

And then Michael and Tora kissed. It was long and soul-felt and Noble – no doubt like most others in the auditorium – had no trouble believing that here were two people who were very much in love.

"Fine! Fine!" said Principal Terashita.

The kiss continued.

"I said *cut*!"

Tora and Michael ended their kiss and looked around strangely, as if they'd momentarily forgotten where they were and what they were doing.

"Was that enough for you, Mr. Greene?" Principal Terashita asked Willie, who had been sitting silently in the front row.

Willie nodded.

"Thank you," said Principal Terashita, ushering Tora and Michael off stage. He glanced at the folded piece of paper in his hand. "Now we have Maria Abruzzo and Brad Horton."

Maria and Brad stepped up onto the stage and took their positions. They would be doing the same scene as Tora and Michael, but already something about the two of them together didn't look right. Brad Horton was a tall, athletic young man with all the features that humans considered handsome; clear skin, good teeth, blue eyes, and high cheekbones. His hair was a little too fine, but the girls in school all liked it well enough. Compared to Brad, Maria looked a little rough around the edges. If he had to pick a word to describe the way she walked, it would be lumbering. Her body was muscular, her skin rough, and her facial features . . . handsome at best. But while Maria had other features that some people found attractive – good figure, thick, dark hair – there was one thing that made her downright ugly. It was her character. Maria was a nasty, mean-spirited girl who would sooner kick you when you were down than offer you a hand up.

Tora and Michael joined Noble, Argus, and Harlan at the back of the auditorium.

"You did good," whispered Argus as he gave Tora's arm a gentle squeeze.

"Nice job," echoed Harlan.

Noble just gave Tora the "thumbs-up" and a wink.

Tora was beaming. She felt it too. She'd done well enough to win the role, the only question now was how good was Maria Abruzzo?

Maria and Brad began the scene. Tora turned away, unable to watch. Noble kept his eyes on the stage. As much as he wanted Maria's performance to be terrible, he had to admit that she was a pretty good actress. She'd obviously rehearsed the scene with Brad Horton over and over. Their timing was perfect, their gestures precise and purposeful, and their performance, on the whole, was charming. Noble glanced over at Tora, who had gathered up the courage to turn back around and watch. Judging by the expression on her face, she thought Maria was good as well. Noble was going to say something comforting, but before he could, Michael put an arm around her shoulders.

Tora sighed, and watched the rest of the scene huddled close to Michael, expecting the worst.

When Maria and Brad were finished, the lights came up and the auditorium buzzed with anticipation.

"First of all," said Principal Terashita. "I just want to thank everyone for trying out. I think we've got an excellent bunch of actors here, and I just know that this year's drama night will be the best one yet. You all deserve a round of applause." He began clapping and everyone joined in, including Willie Greene.

"Mr. Greene," he said. "Would you like some time to make your decisions?"

Willie shook his head.

"Well, all right then," said Principal Terashita, as if he wasn't sure what came next. "I guess I'll hand the show over to you." He laughed at the little joke, but no one else laughed with him. They were all too nervous and anxious to hear Willie Greene make his selections.

"You were all good," he said. "And you each have different qualities that make you ideal for roles in the drama night plays." He paused a moment, as if considering his next words. "The last pair were wonderful and –" he glanced at the clipboard on his lap. "Brad Horton, you'll do well in the role of the young man in *Red Carnations*."

Brad smiled and said, "Thanks."

Maria seemed pleased.

Tora looked crestfallen. If Willie Greene had selected Brad, then Maria was a shoo-in for the role opposite him. After all, they'd been so good together on stage.

"The female lead in that play is a bit trickier because there are two good actors to choose from, but I think –" again he glanced at his clipboard. "– Tora Brock is the better fit."

"What?" Tora said.

"Congratulations," said Noble.

Argus gave Tora a hug. "Yeah, way to go sis!"

Harlan gave Tora a pat on the back.

Michael seemed to be the odd man out.

"Argus," said Noble, tapping his bigger brother on the shoulder. "Hey, Argus!"

Argus stepped back, allowing Michael the chance to offer Tora his congratulations.

Elsewhere in the auditorium, Brad was getting high-fives from all his friends. Maria, on the other hand, was slumped in a chair, arms folded across her chest, with eyes that glared at Tora like a pair of plutonium-powered lasers.

Tora had won the lead in the school play – had won the battle – but, obviously, as far as Maria was concerned, the war was not yet over.

"I'm sorry," Tora said.

"For what?" asked Michael.

Willie Greene had made all of his casting selections and the auditorium was slowly emptying of students. Every once in a while someone would congratulate Tora while others would shake their heads and tell Michael, "tough luck" on their way out.

"You didn't get the part you were trying for."

Michael laughed under his breath. "There's nothing wrong with being Policeman Number Two." Michael had been given a small role with no lines in one of the other drama night plays. "Besides, I'm sure my dad will be proud to see me in a uniform."

"But you rehearsed so hard for the part in *Red Carnations*."

Michael's smile was ear to ear. "I only did that because I got to kiss you each time we reached the end of the play."

Tora was smiling now, too. "I thought that might be the reason."

"Besides, Brad is a way better actor than I'll ever be, and he'll make your performance sparkle."

Tora tilted her head. "So you don't mind that I'll be kissing him during rehearsals, and in front of an audience on drama night?"

Michael considered the question for the longest time. "Of course it's going to bother me, but it'll just be acting, right?"

Tora was silent.

"Right?"

She burst out laughing. "Of course."

"Well it better be." He paused a moment. "Because I'd hate to have to beat the crap out of Brad if he gets any, you know . . . ideas about you and him being an item."

Tora laughed, since Brad Horton was at least a head taller and twenty-five pounds heavier than Michael . . . and had been studying Taekwondo the past six years.

"Hey, I mean it. I'll kick his ass!"

"That's so sweet." Tora leaned forward to give Michael a peck on the cheek when she was bumped from behind. "Hey!" She turned around to find Maria standing there, her hands on her hips and an angry scowl on her face.

"Congratulations!" Maria said through a phony smile.

Tora wasn't sure how to answer. In the end she nodded once and said, "Uh, thank you, Maria."

"I was wondering why your brother was spending so much time talking to Willie Greene the past few days . . . but now I know."

Tora shook her head. "No, it was nothing like that, Maria. Noble and Willie –"

Maria put up her hand like she was stopping traffic. "I don't want to hear it!" she said. "I underestimated you, Tora. I thought you were stupid *and* ugly, but now I know you're just ugly."

Tora could feel the hair along her back begin to bristle.

"And I've always felt there was something weird about you and your brothers, and I mean *really* weird." The right corner of her mouth curled up in a sly, sick sort of smile. "I didn't care all that much before, but now I'm going to find out what it is." When she was done talking, Maria stomped her right foot, spun around on her heel and stormed out of the auditorium.

Tora was left shaken. All of the anger she'd felt toward Maria drained from her body, replaced by a needle of fear. The pack feared no human, but there was something about the tone of Maria's threat that suggested she wouldn't stop until she knew the truth about them. There was going to be a problem . . . a big problem.

"We've got to find Noble," Tora said.

"Why? What for?"

"I've got to talk to him. Right away."

"Relax," said Noble, appearing by Tora's side. "There'll be plenty of time to talk later."

Harlan moved in close to his sister. "Right now, it's time to celebrate your win," he said.

Argus joined them. "With some burgers," he said, rubbing his hands together and licking his lips.

Michael suddenly found himself an outsider, with three

brothers between himself and Tora. "Am I invited to this victory party?" he asked.

The pack turned to Michael.

"Of course, you're invited," said Noble.

Argus put an arm on Michael's shoulder. "Someone has to pay for the food."

The five of them left the auditorium together, laughing and happy.

For now.

Acknowledgments

Writing a novel is always a solitary endeavor, but there are invariably a number of people who assist the author along the way and this is the place to offer them a bit of thanks. And so, thanks, then, to Kathy Lowinger of Tundra Books for believing in the Pack; to Lakeshore Branch Manager, Marilyn Pillar, and the excellent staff of the Innisfil Public Library who helped give this novel its point of origin; to Sergeant Amanda Allen and members of the Peel Regional Police Auxiliary, and their families and friends, who lent their names to a worthy cause – Tyler Allen, Bill Droine, John Hughson, Donna Hughson, Dick Terashita, Brian McAteer, Jake MacKinnon, Willem Grant and Alise Grant; and finally to my wife, Roberta, without whose love and support this book and all my other books would never have been possible.

About the Author

Bram Stoker and Aurora Award-winner Edo van Belkom is the author and editor of some twenty-five books and two hundred stories of horror, science fiction, fantasy, and mystery. As an editor, he's put together two anthologies for young readers, *Be Afraid!* and *Be Very Afraid!*. As an author he's written a previous novel about the pack entitled, *Wolf Pack*. Born in Toronto, he's worked as everything from school bus driver to newspaper reporter, television movie host to prisoner escort officer. Edo van Belkom lives in Brampton, Ontario, with his wife and son.